THE CASE OF
THE CHASED AND
THE CHASTE

BOOKS BY THOMAS B. DEWEY

The "Mac" series:

Draw the Curtain Close
Every Bet's a Sure Thing
Prey for Me
The Mean Streets
The Brave, Bad Girls
You've Got Him Cold
The Case of the Chased and the Chaste
How Hard to Kill
A Sad Song Singing
Don't Cry for Long
Portrait of a Dead Heiress
Deadline
Death and Taxes
The King Killers
The Love-Death Thing
The Taurus Trip

The Pete Schoefield Series

And When She Stops
Go To Sleep, Jeannie
Too Hot For Hawaii
The Golden Hooligan
Go, Honeylou
The Girl With The Sweet Plump Knees
The Girl in the Punchbowl
Only on Tuesdays
Nude in Nevada

The Singer Batts Series

Hue and Cry
As Good As Dead
Mourning After
Handle with Fear

Others Novels

My Love Is Violent
Hunter at Large
Can a Mermaid Kill?
A Season of Violence

THE CASE OF THE CHASED AND THE CHASTE

THOMAS B. DEWEY

WILDSIDE PRESS

CHAPTER ONE

That night, half a dozen of us made up what Bernie Wolf called the "family constellation." We sat in the back section of a motion picture theater in Hollywood. A banner on the marquee had read: Major Studio Preview Tonight.

Bernie Wolf sat on the aisle to my left. On the aisle one row ahead sat Julian Porter, producer of the picture in progress. Beside him was his wife, Carol. The remaining seats in that row were filled by the picture's director, a couple of writers, studio executives and others unknown to me. Most of Julian Porter's "family" were in the row with Bernie and me. They included Louise Reilly, the Porters' housekeeper; Garwood Reilly, her son; and Sophie, the cook. Two other members of the "family" were not present.

The picture was an "outdoor" entertainment, now approaching its climax, and I was enjoying it. Judging by the attentive quiet in the half-filled house, the rest of the audience was doing the same. The only people who were not strictly quiet were those in Julie Porter's row and they were there, not to enjoy the picture, but to appraise it and the audience reaction. To this end, comment cards had been distributed in the lobby.

From time to time, Julie Porter would shift in his seat, looking back, and Bernie Wolf would lean forward to confer with him. Once in a while Bernie would make a note in a small pad. The changing light from the screen gleamed on his horn-rimmed glasses.

There was a vague commotion at the back of the house. When I glanced around, half a dozen so-called "youths" were making their way down the center aisle. They wore leather jackets and they weren't making any effort to be quiet.

Annoyed heads turned to watch. The boys strolled down to the front row and milled around, making a big thing out of selecting seats. They had the entire front section to themselves. There was considerable hissing and shushing from the audience. One by one they sat down.

Bernie Wolf leaned over and spoke in my ear. "I smell trouble. Julie is the one to watch."

I nodded. Bernie straightened in his seat. Julie Porter's big frame twisted nervously.

On the screen, the heroine, one of the most beautiful and persuasive of modern movie queens, was in the throes of a crucial decision. Her lovely, mobile face in close-up nearly filled the wide frame of the screen. The background music was suitably intense.

Suddenly a wolf whistle cut through the carefully sustained mood. I saw Julie Porter jerk in his seat. Breath hissed quietly from Bernie Wolf's mouth. The star's face still filled the screen and the music had softened till it was barely audible. There was a moment of total silence in the audience. Then the front row of seats became a silhouette of harsh, violent action. Arms lifted and swung heavily.

When the first ugly red blob struck the screen, smearing bloodlike streamers over the beautiful face, there was a gasp of outrage from the audience. As others followed, plastering the screen with blotches of red, the reaction changed to silent shock. By then, the front row silhouette had become a file of hunched figures, streaking for the exit door to the left, down front.

The first of them had not reached it when Julie Porter got to his feet. Bernie and I were up a split second later. Bernie plunged down the aisle out of sight. Carol Porter, one hand outstretched, came halfway to her feet. Julie put a hand on her shoulder and whispered urgently. I slid out and Julie banged into me, pushing me aside. We raced each other down the aisle.

The heavy exit door had swung to. As Julie put his weight into it, I stepped on his right heel and we got out there with Bernie. It was an areaway, ten feet wide. Pale light spilled from a small globe over the door. Some more, diffused, came from Hollywood Boulevard and the theater marquee. Two of the six punks leaned casually against the wall. The other four were a hostile cluster in the middle of the passage. One, evidently the leader, stood a little out in front, facing Bernie. He was skinny and frail-looking with hair curled thickly above his ears. He stood in a slight, wiry crouch, his hands in the pockets of his zipped-up jacket.

Julie Porter, with feet planted, elbowed Bernie aside and faced them. His arms were half-raised at his sides, his hands open, the fingers twitching. He started chewing them out in a steady stream of appropriate language, pronouncing all the words distinctly and savagely. As Bernie and I flanked him, the two at the wall stiffened warily.

The skinny punk spat at Julie's feet and snarled back. Julie's hand went up. The kid pivoted, deepened his crouch and brought a knife out of his jacket pocket. The blade was narrow, six inches long, long enough.

"Okay, Fatso," he said. "Like I seen this in a picture once. A little guy with a knife and a big guy. You got a blade, Fatso?"

His closest pals had bunched tight behind him. The two at the wall stepped into the clear, waiting. The sweat on my face was ice-water. Bernie, the youngest of us, was thirty-five, with bad eyes. A pitched battle with six rough teenagers, all of them doubtless armed with something, would be a disaster. Even if we should live through it, we'd be badly cut up. When I remembered Julie's blood pressure, all I could think of was, Stall! Stall and say the right things. Somebody must have called the cops by now!

I edged between Julie and the two loungers and half-faced the one with the knife.

"Only thing to do," I said, "is break this up. There'll be cops here any minute."

I could feel Julie vibrating with rage and braced myself to hold him if he couldn't hold himself. Some of the punks sneered when I mentioned cops, but two of them turned and studied the dark end of the passage where it turned sharp right at a wooden fence. It was their only way out.

One of the loungers swayed toward me, hunching forward.

"Now, Dad, if you want to go a little, like I mean if you're achin' for action…"

The hard, white knots of his fists were stained red. He smelled strongly of overripe tomatoes.

"No action," I said. "I just chickened out."

"What about it, Fatso?" the skinny one was saying. "You chicken too?"

Julie put a hand on my shoulder to push me aside. I backed into him hard and the gang closed in tight. From the corner of my eye I saw Bernie slide his glasses down over his face into his pocket.

"Four-eyes ain't chicken," one of them said. "He took off his cheaters. Lookit!"

"Come on, Four-eyes," the skinny one invited, shifting to show Bernie the knife.

They had spread out now, almost completely ringing us, and I knew the skinny one would go either for Bernie or me at any moment. Julie was pressing me from behind, unable to quit. It left me no room to maneuver. I gave him an elbow in a soft place and he grunted.

"Back off, Julie!" I said.

One of the gang snorted. The skinny one was dancing now, showing off, making short lunges with the knife. Julie backed off a little, but I could still hear him breathing. I felt that Bernie would do what he could, but it wouldn't be much with those eyes, and the punk had reflexes like a fox.

"Like this," I said, talking straight to the knife. "We don't want to fight. And I wasn't bulling about the cops. They're on the way."

Where in hell are they? I thought.

"You hear cops?" one of the punks said. "I don't hear no cops. I hear yellow. All I hear."

The talk was going their way and I hoped they would keep talking. All we would need would be for Julie to make one pass.

The skinny one walked up to me very close. He put the point of the knife in the middle of my chest and held it motionless. Then he spat in my face. All the punks laughed. I took out a handkerchief and wiped my face and by the best stroke of luck in my recent life, both Bernie and Julie stood still for it too.

Skinny backed off, shrugged and turned to his gang.

"I guess he wasn't kiddin', huh? He's chicken. All chicken."

Then we heard the siren, a low growl not far off. The skinny one barked a quiet command. They broke simultaneously and skittered toward the dark end of the alley. They were going over the fence like cats when footsteps pounded behind us and two officers ran up with a strong flashlight.

"What's goin' on?" one said.

Bernie had his glasses on and was pointing toward the wooden fence.

"Six kids," he said. "They just went over the fence."

"Who are you?" the cop asked.

"You want to stand here and talk to us or you want to go after them?" I said.

One of the officers jerked his head at the other and told him to get cruising in the car. He hitched up his belt, checked his holster, got a grip on his flashlight and headed for the fence.

"Good man," Bernie muttered. "You know where my car is. Take Julie home, will you? I'll bring the others."

He walked away. When I turned, Julie was making his way unsteadily toward the Boulevard. After a few steps, he veered toward the wall, planted one hand on it, leaned over and got sick to his stomach. I stood and waited. There was a water tap protruding from the theater building at knee level. I tried to turn it on, but it worked only with a key. I prowled the passage and found a jagged chunk of concrete, about twenty pounds. I carried it back to the wall, lifted it and dropped it on the pipe. The pipe broke and water streamed out. I squatted down and caught it in my hands and washed my face with it for a long time.

Julie got over the sickness and washed his own face and mouth.

"Ready to go?" I asked. "Bernie left his car."

"Okay," he said thickly.

He sat mute in the little car during most of the trip. As I turned in and the front gates swung open and we started up the drive, he said, "How'd you like the goddam picture?"

"Real good," I said. "Up to that time—something happened to the color."

* * * *

An hour later I was sitting in the car with Bernie. He took off his glasses, held them up, found a piece of tissue and polished them methodically, looked through them and put them on. There was a faint tic in the clean, tough line of his jaw. When he wrinkled his forehead, the black hair on his head moved forward and then back, stiffly.

"It's hard to say," he said, "but thanks. If I'd been alone with him out there, somebody would have got killed. Probably Julie."

The front door of the house opened and Louise Reilly came out, carrying a small suitcase and a topcoat. With her was her son, Garwood, a broad-shouldered, thick-chested man of thirty-eight. He swung down the steps expertly on battered crutches. Bernie leaned out of the car.

"Louise?" he called.

They came to the window.

"What time are you leaving in the morning?" Bernie asked.

"I'm not certain," Louise said in her rich trained voice. "Why?"

"Would you give me a ring, please? At home."

"If you wish," she said.

"Thanks."

Garwood Reilly nodded at us. "Sorry about the way things went, Bernie," he said.

"Well," Bernie said, "it could have been worse."

"Disgusting," Louise Reilly muttered. "Ruffians. Rat packs."

"You won't forget to call me, Louise?"

"All right, Bernie."

She put the suitcase and coat into a two-year-old sedan parked on the drive and returned to the house. Gar Reilly glanced at Bernie and looked away.

"You know whether Julie's got around to that script yet?" he said.

"Not yet," Bernie said. "I read it."

"What do you think?"

"Well, Gar, it's kind of late to talk about it."

Reilly shrugged on his crutches. "Okay. The hell with it."

"Don't be like that, Gar," Bernie said. "Go home and get a good night's sleep. I'll call you."

"Okay. So long."

Bernie said nothing more until after Reilly had got in the car and driven away. Then he lit a cigarette and leaned back on the seat.

"What I'm trying to say, I guess, is that I think you may have saved Julie's life."

"Well, my own too," I said.

"I understand." He did some smoking. "I love this Julie," he said. "I've been in the business all my life, working up from the bottom at one of the major studios. I love the business. But it's dying, Mac. You can say there'll always be movies—some kind of movies. But for people like Julie and me, the business is dying in the way we've known it. Julie is like an old bull, trying to cut out a few more heifers before they run him off. Only now—well, who goes to the movies?"

He tossed his cigarette out of the car and looked for a while at the place where it fell.

"I didn't mean to go into a long thing," he said. "You've been around long enough to get the idea. The idea is, Julie can be hurt. You don't see this right away. He's big, loud and tough. But he can be hurt. I've seen him hurt and I don't want to see it any more if I can prevent it. I spend a lot of time trying to prevent it."

He lit another cigarette.

"All I had to say," he said, "you were very good tonight and I appreciate it. So does Julie, but he may never let you know. This is something I would have said to you in the beginning, but I couldn't think of a way. Now I think everything will be all right. Just don't ever hurt him, Mac."

I got out of the car and closed the door silently. Bernie leaned out as I came around.

"And for God's sake," he said, "don't ever tell him what I just told you."

I nodded. "All right, Bernie. Thanks for the talk."

He waved with the lighted cigarette and I went into the house. Carol Porter was just inside the door.

"Has Bernie gone?" she asked.

"Not quite."

She opened the door quickly and went out.

* * * *

It was two in the morning when I got into bed. I didn't hear Bernie drive away nor Carol come upstairs. Not that I listened for them. I spent a long time in the shower, trying to scrub out the memory of that encounter in the alley. Then I stood for a while in the dark at the open window, with the scent of orange blossoms strong in my nose and throat, and finally I turned in.

I kept trying to think things over. I thought about Julie Porter. I thought about Carol Porter, now with Bernie Wolf in the intimate dark—and those other times before. I thought about what Bernie had just been telling me, about Julie and how Julie mustn't be hurt and that devotion and all.

Bernie's was certainly a single-minded devotion. It even worked on his instincts. He had warned me in advance that something was about to happen. Knowing Julie as we both did, we might have played it more sensibly. We might have restrained Julie from going outside to begin with. It was a police matter.

The thoughts kept coming and I kept pushing them away. Unable to fall asleep, I heard a shuffle of footsteps in the hall. I heard them pause, then enter the room next to mine. I saw the pink glow of her night light through the partly open door of her room.

I got out of bed quietly and looked in. Julie Porter was standing beside the satin-canopied four-poster. I saw him lean over, his big frame awkwardly gentle. Straightening with his girl in his arms, he bumped his head lightly against the canopy. She muttered something sleepily and I heard his answering mumble. He carried her, wrapped in bedclothes, across the room and settled down on the floor, holding her. There was another muttered exchange and she put her head against his shoulder and went back to sleep. The black luxury of her hair cascaded over his arm.

Her name was Linda. She was five years old and she had been my specific charge for two weeks.

CHAPTER TWO

She had looked at me with eyes like ripe olives. She had a pale, ascetic face, framed by a lustrous mass of black hair. Her voice was clear and round, bell-like.

"Are you coming out to the Coast to make a picture, Mac?" she asked.

"If I am, I hope you'll help me," I said.

"If I can," she said gravely.

She sat in a window seat, forward in the giant plane, where I had come to meet them in Chicago. Next to her was Alice Rummel, her governess, slim, prim, maybe thirty. Opposite them, sprawled in both seats, sat Julian Porter, motion picture producer, Linda's father, massive and slightly paunchy. His dark, restless eyes worked me over carefully. Rhythmically, almost compulsively, he popped grapes into a mobile mouth, digging them out of a brown paper sack in his lap.

Across the aisle sat Porter's wife, Carol, blond and fur-swathed, and next to her was Bernie Wolf, the man who had called me from their hotel an hour and a half earlier.

Somebody yawned and I said good night and went to my own seat amidships. I had started the trip blind and on short notice, but I had been at liberty, with no reason not to go to California. Now I waited for someone to come and give me a reason not to stay in Chicago.

The job fell to Bernie Wolf, youngish, dark, in horn-rimmed glasses.

"Sony about the rush," he said. "We got this at the hotel, about two hours ago."

He handed me a stamped envelope addressed to Mr. Julian Porter, Palmer House, Chicago. There was no return address. The writing had been done with a rubber stamp outfit that would go at a variety store for sixty-nine cents. The message, on a sheet of white typewriter paper, had been printed likewise.

"Linda Porter," it read, "is a pretty little girl. Keep plenty of cash on hand—you may need it."

I tried to give it back to him, but he told me I could keep it. It felt hot in my pocket.

"Have you told the police, the post-office people?" I asked.

"No. The main thing was protection for Linda. This is the way Julie wants it."

"Julie?"

"Mr. Porter. You'll be calling him Julie. He'll tell you when."

"Just what do you do for Mr. Porter?"

"Anything," he said. "Anything Julie wants done, any time, any place."

"Does he always take his family along on these trips?"

"He always takes me, sometimes his wife."

"Speaking of his wife—"

"Carol, the one you met, is not Linda's mother. That would be Julie's ex-wife, Gen Richards."

"Does he give his present wife an ample allowance?"

He looked at me sharply. "You want to watch that tough talk, boy," he said.

"I want to get the job done," I said.

He took off his glasses and replaced them.

"I guess you'll do," he said. "About the rest of the household—Miss Rummel, the governess, has been checked out clear through the FBI. There's a cook, Sophie, who's been around twenty years. The housekeeper is a Louise Reilly, known Julie for years."

"Any last-minute advice?" I asked him.

"Well—Julie's not hard to get along with. His home runs like a well-oiled sewing machine. I think you'll be comfortable there. Just keep your professional eye on Linda and—oh yes—watch out for Carol."

"Oh?"

"Carol is young, beautiful, restless and easily bored."

He said good night, got up and left me. I sat there with nothing much and pretty soon Julian Porter came back and sat down. He was eating an orange.

"Want one?" he asked. "Stewardess got a crateful." I declined. "I eat all the time," he said. "Ever have ulcers, boy?" I shook my head and we talked about the letter. I suggested he notify the police.

"Look," he said, "I'm what they call newsworthy. Imagine the headlines: Producer's Daughter Threatened. Linda reads some—anyway her own name. Besides—"

"Besides what?"

"Let me put it this way. I want you to track this thing down. How will you go about it?"

"Well, first I'd need a list of names. Everybody you ever said a harsh word to or dealt with. Your ex-wife should be on it, and her associates."

"All right. You'll get a list."

"By the way, does Linda's mother have visiting privileges?"

"No. She's unfit. Court order. She was a lush and she played around." When I said nothing, he prodded me. "Are we clear now? I'm hiring you to check out this letter. And when we catch up with whoever it was, you'll close your eyes while I settle the score. Understand?"

He had the throttle open and the drive was as powerful as any I had ever felt.

"If we get that far," I said, "I'll have to try to prevent you." His eyes were wide and clear against mine.

"How hard would you have to try?" he said.

"Pretty hard, Mr. Porter."

He grinned, slapped my knee and got up.

"I think we're in business," he said. "Call me Julie."

"As you wish," I said.

* * * *

After a while I took a walk forward and checked on my party. They were all apparently asleep. But as I turned to go back, Carol Porter was gazing at me out of sleepy green eyes, fixed, unblinking. I smiled, nodded, touched my hat. She went on looking at me for a moment, then her mouth twitched, her hand rose to cover a yawn and she closed her eyes. Heading for my own seat, I was sharply aware of the throbbing power of the big plane in flight.

CHAPTER THREE

They lived in a two-story house up one of the Sunset Boulevard canyons. There was roughly an acre of tightly fenced grounds. There were a lot of trees, including orange, grapefruit, lemon and avocado; a three-car garage and a swimming pool.

My first view of the interior came as I carried Linda, a limp bundle in my arms, toward a curving staircase, following Miss Rummel's erect, pencil-like figure. To the left of the stairs, a partly open sliding door revealed a breakfast room with floor-to-ceiling windows looking out on the pool. On my right, the living room opened out and under the staircase, in a lounging alcove, were a bar, a sofa, a couple of chairs and some lamps. Carol Porter had already disappeared up the stairs and Julie into a study off the living room.

The upstairs hall was L-shaped, with the turn at the back of the house. This created a balcony overlooking the high-ceilinged reception area of the living room. Miss Rummel opened a door to the left of the head of the staffs and I carried Linda into her own room.

If ever a junior boudoir had been designed, decorated and scented to prove that little girls are made exclusively of everything nice, this was it. Surrounded by Mother Goose wallpaper, assorted stuffed animals, an immense doll collection, satin-covered chairs and a junior-size four-poster, I felt not only ten feet tall but uncouth in the bargain.

I put Linda down and she primped and straightened her skirt with dignity.

"I have to go to the bathroom," she said.

"All right," Miss Rummel said.

"Excuse me, please, Mac?" she said.

"Of course."

She crossed to a bathroom. Through its open doors I could see the room beyond, feminine, but plainer than Linda's.

"Your room?" I asked Miss Rummel.

"Yes," she said. "Yours is right here."

Linda's room had a connecting door leading into mine. My door was at the head of the stairs. The room was small and immaculate, with two windows overlooking a rustic, park-like area between the house and a vine-covered fence. Alice Rummel watched me checking the layout and put a hand to her throat.

"I didn't mean to alarm you," I said. "We have to cover every contingency, even the most remote."

Linda flew into the room and grabbed my hand, tugging.

"Mac, come on!" she said. "I want to show you something."

Alice Rummel spoke with unexpected firmness. "We have to let Mac rest awhile," she said. "Also, we have to do a little resting of our own."

Linda pouted but gave in, looking at me with some suspicion. "Are you going to rest?" she asked.

"I certainly am," I said.

She backed away to her own room. Her suspicion had given way to faint hostility. Alice closed the door behind them. I had opened the suitcase and was lifting out some shirts when the door opened again and Linda looked in. She was wearing blue pajamas with white elephants on them.

"Mac—" she said hurriedly as Alice appeared behind her, "if you want to use my bathroom, just go ahead."

"That's mighty kind," I said, "but I have one of my own, right over there."

"Well," she said, "I mean if yours gets stuck or anything."

"Okay," I said. "A deal."

She backed out of sight. Then I caught a flashing glimpse of her hopping across the room onto her little four-poster. Alice looked in at me with tears in her eyes.

"You won't let anything happen to her, will you?" she said.

"Huh-uh," I said definitely. "Because what if my bathroom should get stuck?"

She blushed faintly, smiled and closed the door. I took off my coat and tie and shoes and lay down. Though early in the morning, it was warm and the air through the open windows was heavily scented. Within minutes I was asleep.

The breakfast room was drenched in sunlight filtered through translucent gold curtains. Through a partly open door, I could see a section of the swimming pool, a cluster of brightly colored umbrellas and chaises longues. Alice and Linda were finishing breakfast. A swinging door opened vigorously and Sophie, the cook, came in, red-faced and breathless. She smelled of flour and milk.

"You like ham and eggs, Mr. Mac?" she said.

"I'm very partial to ham and eggs," I said.

She hovered over Linda, looking worried. "You sure, honey, you don't want more milk?"

"No, Sophie," Linda said. "I'm full."

"You got to get big and strong."

"No, I don't. I'm a girl."

"Girls got to get big and strong, too."

"Strong maybe," Linda said. "Not big."

Sophie looked down at herself happily. "I'm big. Feel fine all the time." She went out, shaking her head.

"She'll put ten pounds a day on you if you let her," Alice Rummel said.

"I'll say this," I said; "you've managed to retain a slender figure."

She looked away. "I guess it's metabolism," she said.

Linda dabbed hastily at her mouth, climbed down and headed out.

"Where are you going?" Alice asked.

"I have to help Watanabe."

"Oh, I don't know—"

"I *have* to! I promised."

Alice looked at me.

"The gardener?" I said.

Alice nodded and I looked around at Linda. "If I come out after breakfast, would you introduce me to Watanabe?"

"All right," she said, "but you better hurry."

She ran out.

"Is the front gate closed?" I asked Alice.

"It's always closed. It works on an electric eye."

Sophie came bustling in with a plate of ham and eggs and half a grapefruit. I fell to, while Alice fingered over her coffee. "You're a registered nurse," I said.

"Yes, how did you know?"

"Just a hunch. You like this work better?"

"It pays better, and it's—yes, I like it. There were things about nursing I never could get used to. Besides, I love Linda."

Outside by the pool there was a scraping sound, metal on concrete. I glanced out. Carol Porter was slipping out of a terry-cloth wrapper. When I looked at Alice again, she was very red and exclusively concerned with the dregs of her coffee. She had been betrayed, in a way. Guest or no guest, Carol hadn't bothered with such nonessentials as a swimsuit.

She was of a breath-taking shapeliness and it would have been foolish of anyone to expect me to close my eyes on such short notice. Miss Rummel may have been that foolish, because as Carol Porter, golden-flanked, long-limbed, poised for her plunge in the sunlight, I felt the shy governess eyeing *me*.

"Excuse me," I mumbled, "you were saying?"

"Nothing," she said. "I couldn't possibly meet such competition."

The blush returned. She pushed back from the table abruptly. "I'd better go check on Linda."

"I'll be right with you," I said.

"Oh, don't hurry," she said. "Just whenever you can manage to drag yourself away."

I was reflecting on how hard it is to know the right thing to do when there were footsteps behind me and I looked around at Louise Reilly, the tall housekeeper. She seemed amused, in her regal way.

"Alice can't quite get used to living with theatrical people," she said. "I hope you'll have less trouble—"

"I'm doing fine," I said, "what with the good treatment and food."

I felt at a disadvantage looking up at her. When I rose, it seemed to take forever to arrive eye-to-eye with her. I decided she had been very handsome and imposing in her day.

"I came from a very strict home," she said. "I daresay a lot stricter than Alice's. My parents never became reconciled to my career on the stage. But I stuck by my guns. In those days you had to."

This could only be the prelude to a session of reminiscing and I just didn't have the time. Nodding pleasantly, I backed off.

"I'm sure you did," I said. "It's a fascinating subject and I hope one of these days you'll find time to tell me about it."

Her face darkened like a lake shadowed by a passing cloud. "I realize you have things to do," she said. "I didn't mean to keep you."

She stalked out as abruptly as Alice had. I was making enemies all over the place. It was clear enough who was to blame and I glowered through the open doorway of the breakfast room. At that moment, Carol came up from the water, breaking high and clean. She caught the edge with her palms, locked her elbows and vaulted lithely onto the blue-and-white thing. Miniature rainbows gleamed in the water drops clinging to her tawny perfection. I watched for a moment as she picked up a towel and scrubbed at her hair, her high, taut breasts shaking lightly with the movement, the tanned flesh of her thighs and buttocks rippling like the pelt of a healthy tigress. As I left the breakfast room, I could feel the throb of that giant plane in memory.

* * * *

In the garage were a station wagon and a red sports car. At the rear of the garage, an outside stairway led to apartments above. There was a TV antenna on top and for the first time I noticed there was no antenna on the main house, nor had I seen a TV set inside.

I spotted my subject trio stooped over a flower bed in the back of the fenced lot. The fence was extra-heavy gauge steel wire on concrete anchored posts, virtually impregnable except by power tools. It gave me a feeling of security. There was an open gate midway along the lot on one side and I crossed over there.

The gate opened on a fifteen-foot setback off the side street that bounded Julie's corner lot. A gardeners truck was parked at the curb. I heard a crunching sound behind me and turned to see Mr. Watanabe, brown and inscrutable, waiting with a wheelbarrow for his turn at the gate. I jumped out of his way, he nodded jerkily and trundled his load outside.

At the rear of the lot, Alice Rummel, on her haunches, was watching Linda set out some small plants. She dug holes with her fingers, splashed water into them liberally, set in the plants and patted the muddy soil carefully—then wiped her hands on her yellow slacks or blouse. Miss Rummel would reach mechanically to brush at them.

"What are they?" I asked innocently.

"Pansies, naturally," Linda said.

"Young lady," Alice said, "you will keep a civil tongue in your head."

"What?"

Alice got up rather stiffly. Linda bounced to her feet, not stiffly at all, and shook her finger at us. "You stay here," she said. "I have to see Watanabe."

Running across the grass toward the side gate she was a windblown flower, slightly dirty. Alice spread her hands.

"How does Linda get to school?" I asked.

Sudden fear shadowed her face. "I take her in the station wagon."

"And pick her up?"

She nodded. I had heard a car on the side street, had noted it without really giving it much thought. Suddenly I found myself watching the gate for Linda's reappearance. I could hear voices—Linda's high and quick; an occasional guttural from Watanabe; then another, different, feminine, low-pitched, unfamiliar. Not Sophie and not Mrs. Reilly.

When I met Alice's eyes, she looked a little flustered. I wondered how she would look under the pressure of having to tell a good strong lie. She wore her emotions like neon signs.

"I think it's just the neighbor from across the street," she said hurriedly.

"I'd like to get acquainted," I said. "You can't know too many people."

I moved toward the gate and she came along reluctantly.

Watanabe was busy at his truck. A dusty sports car had pulled into the curb in front of the truck and a young woman was leaning out of its open window, talking with Linda.

Linda stood first on one foot, then the other, eying Watanabe as if afraid he might sneak off and leave her.

I glanced at Alice, but it didn't help any.

Beside the woman in the car, a young man sat slumped behind the wheel. They looked somewhat alike—brother-sister alike. But the brother was a healthier, better-looking man than his sister was a woman.

Linda caught sight of us and grabbed the chance to escape. She flung herself away from the car and dodged past us through the gate. "'Bye, I have to go," she called.

"Goodbye, Linda," the woman said quietly.

Her eyes remained on the place where Linda had disappeared; hungrily, I thought. The young man behind the wheel straightened up and started the motor. Slowly, the woman's eyes swung to Alice, then to me. Alice was deeply flushed.

"Hello, Miss Rummel," the woman said.

Alice moved to the car and I went along. "Hello," she said, "Gen—Miss Richards—this is—Mac."

"Hello," I said.

"And Miss Richards' brother, Paul," Alice said.

"Hi," the young man said, leaning over the wheel.

A bell rang. Paulie Richards. A flashy West Coast fighter. There was a nickname—I couldn't remember. I nodded to him.

"Go now, Gen?" he said.

"All right, Paulie."

The little car moved off down the street. I looked at Watanabe, who was still busy around the truck, his face brown and inscrutable as always. I wondered what his schedule was. Probably at least twice a week he was in and out of this gate, with Linda frequently helping him. With now and then some diversion, such as a sports car with a couple of people in it, pausing to pass the time of day. Always the same car?

I followed Alice into the yard. Down at the end, Linda was at her planting.

"Julie's ex-wife?" I asked.

Alice nodded.

"How often does Watanabe come?"

"Twice a week."

"Always in the morning?"

"No, usually in the afternoon."

"After Linda gets home from school?"

"Yes," she said reluctantly.

We were strolling toward the back of the lot and she stopped suddenly. She underwent a kind of stiffening and when she looked at me, it was straight on. "Will Julie—Mr. Porter have to know?" she asked.

I gave her a minute for bracing.

"He'll have to know what I know," I said, "to the extent that it bears on my job. I guess I'll have to be the judge of that."

She didn't flush, nor fluster, nor blush. She stood there for about thirty seconds, looking at me, then nodded once. "All right," she said. "Thanks for being honest about it."

She turned and started across the grass toward the busy little gardener.

She'll do, I thought, following her. She's tough in the head.

CHAPTER FOUR

When I told Julie, he didn't react as I expected. He hardly reacted at all. We were in his study. Julie slumped in a swivel chair behind his massive, littered desk. Bernie lounged on a sofa. It was about eight o'clock in the evening. As the only report I had for that first day concerned the surreptitious visit by Gen Richards, I made it bluntly and got it over with.

Julie sat still for about three minutes. Then he went to the door, yanked it open and yelled for Louise Reilly. She didn't appear immediately and Julie returned to his desk. When she came in, he was under good control.

"About this thing of Gen coming around to see Linda," he said.

Without exactly moving, Louise drew herself up. "As I understand it, Julie," she said, "I am the housekeeper here, not the watchdog."

"Louise," Julie said mildly, "you're a wonderful housekeeper. This house runs like a top and don't think I don't appreciate it."

"Thank you," she said.

"All right. Now what in the hell is this about Gen sneaking around here to see Linda?"

"I know nothing about it and don't speak to me in that way."

Julie sighed and slumped in his chair. "Louise," he said, "I don't want to get in your hair. You know your lines. Which role you want to play tonight? Take your time, don't hurry. Go ahead whenever you're ready. Bernie, provide a little background music." Julie picked up a pencil and made a baton of it. "Here we go, quietly now—I came to this fair city—

Louise Reilly maintained her full dignity. Julie dropped the pencil, ran his hands through his hair, then spread them in supplication above the desk. "Louise, you're not *helping* me!"

"I can't," she said. "Nobody can help you."

Julie sat up and his tone was brisk again. "All right," he said, "but I don't want Gen on this property, or hanging around here. So you know."

"Is that all?" she asked.

"Yeah, yeah, for God's sake. That's all!"

She started out.

"Louise," Bernie said, "how about if I look at your television this evening?"

She gave him a measured glance. "It is not my television. It is Sophie's."

"Well, you share the sitting room, I didn't want to barge in—"

"I have asked Sophie more than once to move the television into her bedroom."

Julie was scowling at his desk.

"If you're worried about inconveniencing me," Louise said, "don't give it another thought. If it's all right with Sophie, it's all right with me. I'll be out, watching a movie."

"Good girl," Bernie said, "thanks."

"Why don't you wait a few days and see a *good* movie?" Julie said. "I've got a preview coming up. I'll see you get tickets. For free."

"I can hardly wait," Louise said.

"So go," Julie said amiably.

She went out. Julie chuckled and settled back in his chair. "What an actress!" He sobered, looking at me. "She really was, in her day. Terrific. On the stage." He shook his head sadly. "In pictures—nothing. She was scared of the camera." I thought for a minute he had forgotten what he had started with, but in the next breath he said, "Did Linda know who she was talking to?"

"I don't know," I said. "She seemed anxious to get away."

He nodded with satisfaction. "I don't know how long it's been going on, but let's put a stop to it."

"Of course, you can't keep Gen off a public street," Bernie said.

Julie looked at me. "Any ideas?" he said.

"I guess we could keep Linda off the public streets," I said.

"No—don't curtail the kid. We'll change Watanabe's hours. Let him come in the morning when Linda's in school. The rest of the time, keep the damn gate locked. Okay?"

"Okay," I said. "About the school—"

"That time is your own," Julie said. "They've got their own man on the school. Good man."

"How much of a drive is it for Alice Rummel, each way?" I asked.

"Couple of miles. You want to take that over? Then you could use the station wagon while Linda's there—"

"If it won't upset Linda," I said.

Julie's face twisted broadly. "To get escorted to school by a man? Boy, you watch that girl's nose—take a block and tackle to get it down."

"She goes for older men," Bernie said.

Julie started laughing. "She already made Bernie promise to wait for her. You know something—I think he meant it. Huh, Bernie?"

"It wouldn't be the first time a guy married the boss's daughter," Bernie said.

Julie picked an orange out of a bowl on his desk and peeled it, chuckling. "Let's see, when she's eighteen, you'll be—how old, Bernie? Eighty-seven?"

"Come on," Bernie said.

"Too long to wait," Julie said, shaking his head. "Better get out of it. But let her down easy, boy, huh?" He looked at me. "No kidding, Mac, she's in love with Bernie. If I ever saw it."

"Well," Bernie said, "tomorrow it will be Mac. I can see the signs. All through dinner, she hardly looked at me."

"She's worth fighting over," I said.

"You know it," Bernie said.

Chuckling, Julie lifted some papers from his desk and tossed them at me. "That list you asked for," he said.

I picked it up and it consisted of ten pages, single-spaced, one name per line. Both Julie and Bernie were watching me.

"Of course, that's only the start," Julie said. "It takes a little time."

He seemed very amused.

"I'll try to keep it under ten thousand," Bernie said. "Names, I mean."

I took out the rubber-stamped letter Bernie had given me on the plane the night before, opened and glanced at it and held it up for the two of them to look at.

"Everybody has his own job," I said. "You got this letter, then you got me. There may be nothing here. It may be a gag—a ghoulish kind of retaliation by some psychotic nursing a grudge. That seems likely, because the way this is written, there's no concrete demand—no way the letter writer can gain anything, like money. All he could get from this would be the knowledge that you were being driven a little crazy. A good neurotic might get some secret satisfaction out of that.

"So maybe there's no real threat to Linda at all, no intention to harm her. But we don't know, do we? And as long as we don't know, we can't take any chances. We have to have constant protection for Linda. At two-fifty a week, that's great for me. I could hang around two, three years, living high and driving Linda to and from school. A dream of an assignment. And, after what I've just said, about one cut above blackmail.

"On the other hand, if I could break the case, get the answer and eliminate the threat—maybe a couple of weeks, a couple of months—"

Julie was nodding. "See what you mean," he said.

"As far as the list goes," I said, "even if it's a long one, you have to understand I don't expect to ring every doorbell and make up a dossier for everybody on it. Most of the people would be in the business, am I right? Actors, writers, technical people—and as I also understand, practically all of them are tightly organized. That means records—addresses, telephone numbers, present whereabouts. Without too much trouble, we get the organizations to co-operate. We eliminate names in blocks, not just one at a time. A lot of these people would be out at a glance—dead, or moved away, or out of the business."

There was some silence and Julie looked at Bernie, waiting, then said quietly, "All right, Bernie? Any objections?"

"No," Bernie said. "No objections."

"What kind of help do you want?" Julie asked.

"One man. Somebody to watch Linda while I'm out and—vice versa. Part-time only."

"Want me to get one of the agencies?" he said, reaching for the phone.

"If it's all the same to you, I have a couple of contacts out here."

"Okay," he said.

There was a knock at the door. Julie barked something. The door opened and Mrs. Reilly looked in. She was wearing a hat and topcoat, carrying a purse.

"Well?" Julie said.

"May I assume it will be all right for me to go out for the evening now?" she said.

Julie bowed solemnly. "Certainly, Miss Bernhardt. Have a ball for yourself."

She lifted her nose, closed the door quietly and disappeared. Bernie looked at his watch.

"Anything else before the meeting?" Julie asked.

He was scowling deeply and I had the feeling he wanted Bernie not to leave.

"I'll find Sophie," Bernie said, "and see if she'll let me look at the TV—"

The door flew open. Linda sailed into the room, trailing organdy, her black hair bouncing on her shoulders. She ran straight to Julie and he caught and swept her onto his lap in one smooth motion.

"Look what I found!" she said.

I glanced around, and Alice Rummel was looking in from the open door. She shrugged at me and left.

"All right," Julie said, "big entrance, big deal. So what did you find?"

Linda laid her treasure on the desk in front of him. Julie stared at it, then at me. Bernie moved slowly toward the desk and I joined him.

What she had found was a piece of rubber type, such as comes with a stamp outfit. I looked down at the letter in my hand, folded it and put it away.

Linda, on her father's lap, was examining the little cube, turning it over and over with her fingers. Bernie and I leaned across the desk.

"See, it's a letter," she said. "I had a whole bunch of them—and a thing, you know—" she clenched her fist and made a banging gesture—"to put them in and you can write with it!" She looked up at us with that look. "They got lost," she said. "All but this one. I found it."

"Where did you get them?"

"Huh?"

"When you had a whole bunch. Where did you get them?"

"For my birthday, remember?"

"Last year?"

"Certainly. I haven't had this year's birthday yet."

"When did you lose them?"

"I don't know. I know they got lost."

"For sure?" Julie said.

"Certainly," she said haughtily.

Alice Rummel came into the room.

"Who gave them to you?" Bernie asked Linda.

"What?"

"For your birthday. You said it was a present. Who was it from?"

She frowned, faying to remember, then shrugged. "I don't know. I forget."

Julie and I looked at Alice. She spread her hands. Julie hugged Linda and set her on her feet.

"You leave it here," he said, "and maybe somebody will give you another set just like it."

"For my birthday?"

"Why not? So go to bed, baby."

Alice put a hand on her shoulder.

"Night," Linda said.

"Good night, doll."

"Night, Bernie. Night, Mac."

We said good night and she and Alice went out. Julie and Bernie and I exchanged looks.

"When was her birthday?" I asked.

"A year ago," Julie said. "She'll be six in about two weeks."

I took the letter out again and tried to compare the block letters with Linda's lone piece of type. "One letter wouldn't mean much," I said. "Besides, they turn these things out by the thousand."

I folded the type into the letter and put it in my pocket. Bernie was looking at his watch again and Julie caught him at it. Something was happening inside Julie. His breathing was heavy and irregular, his face distorted. When he looked up at Bernie, he was glaring.

"All right!" he exploded. "Go look at your stinking little box! Enjoy yourself! Here—" he jerked open a desk drawer—"you want a pair of binoculars so you can see better? Maybe Sophie will give you one of those stinking TV dinners all squeezed up in a stinking cellophane package you can eat off your stinking lap while you watch the lousy squished-up little postage stamp of a stinking screen—go ahead! Get the hell out of here."

Bernie looked at him calmly from behind the big glasses. His brown eyes resembled those of a deer.

"It's publicity, Julie," he said. "We can use it. I'll drop in after."

"Sure," Julie said. "Drop in. Tell me how it looked. I'll hold up a stinking reading glass so I can see your lips move."

"Okay," Bernie said. "Good night, Mac. I'll be in touch with you tomorrow."

"Thanks, Bernie," I said.

He picked up a thick briefcase and went out, opening and closing the door with deliberate quiet. Julie glared after him, then slumped in his chair.

"Television," he muttered.

"If you'll excuse me," I said, "I'll make the rounds and turn in."

"Sure," he said. He came violently alive again, lifted a stack of paperbound manuscripts. "Here, take along some scripts. Read yourself to sleep. Tell me what you think." He dropped the stack on the desk. "Excuse me," he muttered. "I've got three good pictures in there. Three real good ones. And I'm only going to make one. You know why?"

I nodded.

"Why?" he said.

"Television."

I was prepared for him to explode again, but he didn't.

Instead, he smiled, a little one-sidedly and relaxed in his chair. It squeaked under him.

"Okay, Mac," he said. "Go do whatever you have to do. We can always talk about television."

"Is the mechanism on the front gate in good shape?" I asked.

"Yeah," he said. "Had it fixed last week. Works like a clock. Which in fact it is."

I started out, hesitated at the door. "Incidentally," I said, "I'd be interested in reading the scripts. Any time they're available."

He spread his hand magnanimously. "Help yourself. When you feel like it."

I nodded to him and went out. Carol Porter, in a tight fitting, one-piece coverall, was curled up on a sofa, reading. She glanced at me and nodded and I waved at her on my way out through the breakfast room.

* * * *

THE CASE OF THE CHASED AND THE CHASTE | 27

It was a balmy night. Some of the orange trees were in bloom and the fragrance was heavy on the warm air. I had a flashlight I had found in the garage and I checked the fence all around and the lock on the back gate. Returning, as I made my way toward the house again, I looked up at the windows of the garage apartments. Lights came on in a room on the right and I saw Sophie's generous figure move past them, pause and draw the shades. There was a very dim light in the next, middle room, and I guessed that was the location of the TV set. The bedroom on the left, dark now, would be Louise Reilly's. I pictured the walls covered with photographs and mementos of her theatrical career.

I went through the garage, past Julie's big black Cadillac and Carol's red sports car and down the drive toward the front yard, checking the fence as I went. The kitchen was dark when I passed, but the lights were still up in Julie's study toward the front of the house.

The front fencing was as tight as the rest of it and the imposing gate tightly locked. So I felt a little silly at the painstaking check. But it was part of the routine. You could let it go and maybe nothing would ever happen. But if something should…

I walked down the narrow strip of lawn below the bedroom windows. Above, my room and Linda's were dark. Lights were on in Alice Rummel's room and the shades were discreetly drawn. I went on to the small gate opening onto the patio and swimming pool. The gate was locked.

It seemed early to turn in. I strolled around the front yard, taking in fresh air and stretching my legs. Bernie's yellow MG was parked on the drive at the front door. I walked around it, admiring it. I walked down to the gate and looked through it for a while at the empty street. The fragrance of orange blossoms was almost cloying in my nostrils.

After ten or fifteen minutes, there being nothing more to check up on, I went back to the garage and replaced the flashlight on a shelf. Earlier, I had heard the television upstairs, low and muffled, but now it had been turned off. I went out by a side door and walked the rim of the silent pool. At the far end, light from the house made a dull glow over the lounging area with its umbrella tables and chaises longues. Two of the chaises were occupied. There had been low voices for a moment when I left the garage; now there was silence. Light gleamed dully on Bernie Wolf's glasses. Beside him, stretched out, lay Carol Porter. Their heads were very close together. It was none of my damn business.

CHAPTER FIVE

After seeing Linda safely to school, Alice Rummel and I rode down to Wilshire Boulevard in Beverly Hills and went into a coffee shop. I looked at her across the table and decided she would be a worthy challenge to a man with the time to take it up. Behind her stiff reserve, she was not unpretty, but she had an air of being oppressed by a vaguely unpleasant odor.

"Thank you," she said, "for what you told Julie—or didn't tell him."

"How did you know?"

"I'd have heard about it at once—in a loud voice."

"I had nothing to do with it," I said. "You weren't responsible for Miss Richards' coming around."

"No, but I closed my eyes to it. I let it go on."

"Well, it's all right now. Watanabe's hours have been changed."

She ran a slim, unpainted fingertip around the rim of her coffee cup. "It's too bad—" she said.

"About Miss Richards?"

"After all, she's the girl's own mother."

"What happened with her?"

She blushed. Pretty soon she said, "You understand, I wasn't there. I was hired after they separated."

"I understand. You don't like to serve warmed-over gossip."

"That's a good way to put it."

"Well, it's just between the two of us and in my business, everything may help. I don't expect you to spell out every messy detail."

She drank some coffee and made her decision. "They were married about a year before Linda was born. I don't know how they met. I think it had something to do with her brother. He's a—boxer?"

"A prize fighter. I know."

"I think Mr. Porter had what they call—an interest?"

"A piece of him."

She blushed faintly and nodded. "Anyway, it seems that shortly after Linda was born, there was a party. One of those—parties. Everyone thought Mr. Porter was out of town. But if he was, he returned unexpectedly."

I see.

"As you know, Mr. Porter is quick-tempered."

"I've noticed. But he cools off quickly and he seems fair-minded."

"Yes, but there had been other occasions and—Miss Richards was somewhat alcoholic. Then you have to understand how Julie—Mr. Porter feels about Linda."

"Didn't Miss Richards put up any fight for custody or visitation?"

"I think she was in no position to put up a fight for anything."

"Do you happen to know whether Julie pays her any alimony? Enough to satisfy her needs?"

"I believe he made a flat settlement."

"So she—and her brother—may be hard up."

She halted her cup in midair. "What do you mean by that?"

"Well, if there was a way to extort money from Julie by using Linda as the lever, one way to go about it would be to set up a thing like coming around and winning the kid's confidence. Then, one day—" The horror in her face stopped me.

"I'm just being hypothetical," I said.

"I know. But kidnapping! Even Gen Richards wouldn't—"

"I don't say she would. But if she should, a jury would probably go very light on an unfortunate mother kidnapping her own natural daughter. They might not consider it kidnapping at all."

She looked away, her face clouded. She didn't like the idea, possibly because of her own passive implication. I couldn't blame her. She looked at her watch.

"I'm sure there are things you'd like to do," I said. "If you have one more minute—how about this rubber stamp outfit?"

"I wish I knew," she said. "I've wracked my brain."

"You don't remember who gave it to her?"

She shook her head.

"Do you remember when she discovered it was lost?"

"Not exactly. She has so many toys—She was asking about it several days ago. We looked all over for it. I could hardly remember her having had it at all. She never used it."

"*Never* used it?"

"Just at first, a few times. The letters didn't mean much to her then."

"And you can't put your finger on specific dates for any of this?"

"No. Only that last night was when we found that one piece."

I nodded. "I don't want to keep you," I said. "Thanks for talking with me."

We walked outside and she said she would go home by taxi when she had finished her shopping. I would pick Linda up in the station wagon after school.

* * * *

I found a telephone and dialed an old number. The number had long since been changed, but the rumbling voice that answered the new one was as familiar as the sound of the Chicago River against the Wacker Drive pilings.

"How's the Mick?" he asked.

I told him how Donovan was. They had made a great team in the old days; the "Mick" and the "Hunky"—Donovan and Walewski to all but each other. The big Pole was a few years older and had been retired against his deepest wishes. Idleness was bad enough for him anywhere, but idleness in Chicago, where he had been born and served his time, was impossible. Now, on the south side of Los Angeles, he owned a house he had built with his own hands.

I remembered his hands. I had seen him lift the front end of a pickup truck high enough to free Donovan's trapped leg after a berserk plumbing contractor had run him down. I had been a spectator because someone had to cover the plumber and I couldn't lift the truck. Afterward, Walewski hadn't been troubled by so much as a sore muscle. Talking to him now I had the sudden thought that, very possibly, Walewski would never die except by accident—like an atomic explosion.

I told him I needed some part-time help.

"Well," he said, "I got plenty to do. I got to set on my can a certain amount of time to get up strength enough to turn on the TV. But if you need help—" Actually, he was overjoyed. I asked him to come out to the Porter house between two and four in the afternoon when Linda would be taking her nap, and we could talk.

"If I can make it," he said. "I got to take care of myself. If it wasn't for power steering—" I hung up laughing.

I went to a variety store and looked into the rubber stamp situation. There was nothing much to see in it. A clerk looked at my sample of type and found a complete outfit of a similar size. There was no way to tell whether the sample matched it or one of half a dozen other brands. I bought the set, so someone could give it to Linda for her birthday.

I parked the station wagon on a quiet, tree-lined street not far from Linda's school. There was a small park and I sat on a bench and looked at Bernie's list and tried to formulate some procedures for dealing with it.

He had it well classified. Actors, actresses, producers, directors, writers, script girls, stenographers and some other categories were included. He had crossed out four names and written "deceased" in the margin. It didn't amount to much reduction. I looked at the names without expectation. The project had never been more than a leave-no-stone-unturned type of thing, even in my mind. But when Julie and Bernie had thrown it at me with that sly, half-joking challenge, I hadn't had much alternative but to take it in stride. With Walewski to help me, we could at least dispose of it in a short time.

I folded it into my pocket and walked around for a while in the quiet, rich, well-run town, and at one-fifteen I drove to the school to meet Linda. She was romping full tilt with half a dozen other junior citizens when I went to the gate. When she saw me, she left her friends and ran to me as if she had been discharged by a cannon.

She was silent during the ride home, until we turned the last corner and could see the gate up ahead. Then, looking at me gravely, she said, "If anybody should try to kidnap me, would you stop them?"

The steering wheel jumped in my hand.

"I sure would," I said. "But nobody's going to try that."

"Oh, they might," she said.

"Not while I'm around," I said.

"But what if you couldn't stop them?"

"Well, if I couldn't, Bernie would. And if he couldn't, Julie would."

"Sometimes even the police can't stop them."

I turned into the entrance and watched the big gate swing open.

"What made you think about this—kidnapping thing?" I asked her.

She shrugged, looked away and out the window. "Oh, I don't know. I just thought of it."

"Well, what do you say we think about something else?"

"Okay," she said and got out of the car.

I waited till she had opened the door and gone in, before rolling slowly around to the garage and putting the car away.

A little later, sitting under an umbrella beside the pool, I found it very difficult to keep my mind on anything Walewski was saying. I had given him the picture and shown him Bernie's list and we had worked out a system in which we would share the leg work and he would be on call in case I should need him to watch Linda. Afterward, he had got to reminiscing. He was a good reminiscer and at any other time it would have been a pleasure. But Linda's question crowded my mind and finally, as gently as I knew how, I got him to take his leave.

* * * *

That night, around midnight, Linda woke up screaming. Alice Hummel and I got to her bedside at about the same time, but when we asked her about the bad dream, she wouldn't talk about it. She wanted me to stay with her. I sat down beside the bed and she held tightly to my hand for a long time and finally she went to sleep.

CHAPTER SIX

Twelve days passed. Linda didn't mention kidnapping again and neither did I—to anyone. It was the sort of idea she might have picked up around school or heard over the radio, maybe in a newscast. She might have heard it long ago and just recently got to thinking about it. I had no reason on the evidence to think that anyone in the household had mentioned it to her. If I had told Julie, he'd have pressed for a shakedown and that would certainly have got back to Linda. Besides, Julie had problems of his own. The preview was coming up and plans were being laid in quiet corners for Linda's birthday party three days later.

Walewski and I worked on the list, and got nowhere, except that we eliminated a lot of names. Bernie kept giving us additional ones and tried to fill in background on them, but some he barely knew.

Around noon on the day before the preview, I got a call from Bernie at home.

"You asked me once," he said, "what my job is. What I'm supposed to do for Julie?"

"I remember."

"Well, if your relief man is available, come on over and hang around."

I called Walewski and lined him up to be on hand when Linda would get home from school. At about two o'clock I drove over to Bernie's house. His MG was parked in front and he had me put the station wagon in the garage and closed the door.

His place was a bachelors haven, small, comfortable and masculine, set in a deep canyon in quiet surroundings. His nearest neighbor was four blocks down the road. He got out a bottle of brandy and some glasses, set them on a small stand beside a high-backed leather armchair and settled into it.

"You've heard about the so-called Hollywood yes-man," he said.

"Sure."

"Well, I'm a no-man. I get to say 'no' at the proper times, regardless of what Julie has already said. This is against my nature. I had to learn how. What I really get paid for is to be in that place where everybody who wants something is bound to think, 'I could deal with Julie Porter all right, if it wasn't for that son of a bitch, Bernie Wolf.'"

I nodded. I couldn't see exactly what it had to do with me, but he served a very good brandy.

"I have a hunch," he said, "that's a predicament you might understand."

I nodded again.

"Maybe sometimes I get a little lonesome," he said. "Anyway, a lot of this 'no' business I do at home. I will probably be doing some this afternoon and I thought you might like to overhear it."

There was no need for me to confirm his suspicion. I wished he had felt like expressing the real motive behind the invitation—I knew Bernie well enough by now to know he never did anything without a reason—but I didn't expect an advance explanation. With Bernie, you were on your own.

We talked some about the weather and the upcoming baseball season and other odds and ends. From time to time, Bernie consulted his watch. At about two-forty-five, he took me into a small den off the living room where he had a desk, a typewriter and stacks of books, magazines and manuscripts.

"Make yourself comfortable," he said. He half-filled my medium-sized brandy snifter. "Will that do for a while?"

"If it doesn't…" I said.

He grinned a little. It was rare in him.

"You have a refreshingly close mouth," he said. "I work in a business full of great talkers. How they talk."

On his desk was a modest bronze plaque. I could read Bernie's name on it, but that was all.

"May I?" I asked, reaching for it.

Bernie shrugged. I picked it up and read: *To Bernie Wolf—For Outstanding Services—1956—West Side Youth Council.* "Good for you," I said. "Still doing it?"

He shrugged again. "It's about the extent of my public service," he said. "We set up a kind of weekend camp out in the Valley. A little movie equipment, one thing and another. We pick up a wagonload of these kids every so often and go out there. It's a drop in the bucket, but sometimes you get to some of them."

"How tough do they come?"

"Not too tough. You don't get far with the real mean cases, partly because you don't get the chance till they're in bad trouble. By then they've had the cops and the courts. I've seen a lot of them. Some you wouldn't touch with a long pole, you know? They need other help."

Outside there was the sound of a car as it pulled in, idled and went silent. Bernie backed off with the bottle.

"Keep your ears open," he said. "You might pick up some interesting material this afternoon."

I raised my glass. "To the ancient and honorable practice of snooping," I said.

He grinned and went out, leaving the sliding door open about an eye's width. I moved a chair silently and when I sat down, I could see the corner of the living room that contained Bernie's chair, the little stand and, beyond, the kitchen door. I heard him open the front door and speak.

"Hello, Gen—Paulie—" His voice was unexpectedly gentle. "Drink, Gen?"

"Thanks, Bernie."

"Paulie?"

"Never touch it," Paulie said.

I suddenly remembered the nickname he went by. "Velvet Gloves." An exuberant sports columnist, describing one of Paulie's fights, had written, "The young man with the velvet gloves literally caressed his opponent into oblivion in round five." The sentence had been deleted from later editions, but the moniker had stuck.

I had seen neither brother nor sister since that first morning and while Bernie was in the kitchen, mixing a drink, and Paulie prowled the room like an adolescent panther, I studied Gen Richards.

I guessed her age as thirty, though her hairdo and dress were those of a teen-ager. There were traces of a winsome prettiness that must have been very appealing when Julie had first met her. But now the ravages of her particular neurosis showed plainly and her face resembled that of an actress made up for Stella Dallas. She sat very still in her chair with her hands folded, and her knuckles were white. When Bernie brought her the drink, she held it with both hands, as if afraid someone would take it away from her. But she drank slowly, in small sips.

"So how are things?" Bernie asked easily, sinking into his chair.

Paulie stopped his pacing. "We want to see Julie," he said abruptly.

"Have you called him?" Bernie asked.

"Oh, come on," Paulie said.

"What's it about?"

Gen turned her glass slowly in her hands, studying the amber contents. "I'm afraid it's about money, Bernie," she said.

"Oh?" Bernie glanced up. "No fights coming up, Paulie?"

"Whenever the Commission gets off its ass," Paulie said. "I can't fight the referees."

Bernie turned back to Gen, waiting. She played with the glass and drank some and then looked at him.

"Also," she said, "it's about Linda."

"I see," Bernie said. "What about Linda?"

"I think I've served my time, Bernie," she said stiffly. "After all, she's my own daughter."

Bernie just kept watching and waiting.

"I don't mean I expect the whole thing at once—"

"The whole thing?"

"I mean—not custody or anything. Just reasonable visitation."

"She means *legal*," Paulie cut in harshly. "Without sneaking around the back door. By the way, who is that guy hanging around there now? We see him one day, the next day—all closed up. Gen hasn't seen Linda for two weeks. What's he—some kind of cop?"

"He's a writer," Bernie said smoothly. "He's shaping up a script with Julie."

"A writer," Paulie said.

"Listen, Bernie," Gen said, "don't you think it's fair, by this time, I should at least get to see her sometimes?"

Bernie poured himself some brandy and took time to swish it around. "Do you have an attorney?" he asked.

"Let's knock off the sparring routine," Paulie said. "We're broke. Julie made a very fast deal with that settlement. If he won't come through with something for Gen, we'll take it to court."

"You too, Gen?" Bernie asked quietly.

She looked into her empty glass with a kind of hopelessness. "I think it's only fair that I should get to see Linda," she said.

Bernie set down his glass, got up and looked out a window. Paulie Richards looked at his sister and she looked into her empty glass.

"I'll tell Julie you need something," Bernie said. "Frankly, I don't think he'll be interested."

"He'd better be interested," Paulie said, raising his voice. "We've got plenty on Julie—"

Bernie turned around. "No, you haven't, Paulie," he said. "Don't try to bull your way through this. Let me give you some advice. Don't ever try to get to Julie through Linda. The same goes for me. Don't make threats."

"It was no threat!" Paulie yelled.

"When you tell me you're broke," Bernie said, "I understand it. When Gen tells me she wants to see Linda, I understand that too. There's nothing dirty in either one of those. But when you tell me in one breath that you want money and in the next breath that Gen ought to have visitation rights, that's dirty. If I don't go for it, you think Julie will go for it? Not in court or anywhere else. And if you can find a judge who will go for it, Julie will get him thrown off the bench, and I'll help."

Paulie Richards was on his toes, rigid, eying Bernie. Gen got up slowly and put her glass down on the stand.

"We'd better go, Paulie," she said. "Bernie will do what he can.

She had lost and she knew it, if Paulie didn't. But she had lost so many times there could hardly be anything new in the experience.

Bernie watched them go. At the door, Paulie turned for a parting shot, sheer bluster type.

"Just think it over real hard, Bernie," he said. "There are ways."

"Goodbye, Paulie," Bernie said. "I think you'd be happier if you could scare up a fight."

"Never mind that. Talk to Julie. If you don't, I will."

"All right, Paulie."

They went out. Bernie picked up his brandy glass, stared into it, then opened a sliding door and stepped out onto a small patio. I saw him take some of the brandy, roll it around in his mouth and spit it out on the grass. He looked at his watch.

Is it them? I kept thinking. Could it be them?

Bernie had disappeared. I heard the Richards' car turn and go away. Then within three or four minutes, another car approached, pulled up in front of the house and stopped. I found a hairline opening in the closed drapes and looked out. A car door slammed. A moment later, I saw Garwood Reilly come around the corner of the front hedge and down the walk. He had the massive chest and shoulder development of the paraplegic and propelled himself with long, sure strokes of his crutches, barely touching the ground from time to time with his useless feet.

The doorbell sounded a quiet bell tone and Bernie crossed the room to let him in. There was a mumbled greeting. Reilly slid onto an armless chair, racked his crutches beside him and leaned on them. He declined the drink Bernie offered.

"You'd be easier to get along with, Reilly," Bernie said, "if you'd develop a few vices."

Reilly chuckled with the appreciation of the connoisseur. "One up," he said. "That's good for you, Bernie. First thing you know, Julie will stick you in the genius department."

"I guess I'm still one up," Bernie said dryly. "What's on your mind?"

"You know me—always busy, working every minute. I brought some revised pages for that horror picture you're sitting on."

"I wouldn't exactly say we're sitting on it, Gar."

"Well, hell, Bernie, you've had it for over a month."

"It's on Julie's desk."

"You haven't read it yet either?"

"Not yet. We've been fighting this thing for the preview tomorrow. If you'd like it back, to try somewhere else—"

"Okay, hatchet man," Reilly said. "Is that the word now? Knock off, Reilly?"

"Easy, boy."

"Look, Bernie. I can get fifteen hundred a week for TV crap."

"That's better than Julie can do for you. Why don't you go ahead?"

"Come on—let's be loyal!"

"You be loyal. I'll make a buck where I can."

There was a pause. Reilly shifted his crutches to the other side of the chair and looked at Bernie cautiously.

"You were never a dependable straight man," Reilly said. "How do I take that remark?"

Bernie shrugged. "You know how the business is," he said.

"No fooling, is Julie going to pull out?"

"Not Julie."

There was some more silence. Very offhand, Reilly slid his hand up the crutches and back down.

"Had some good offers, Bernie?" he asked.

"Nothing fabulous."

"How fabulous would it have to be?"

"Well—you know, it wouldn't be easy to leave Julie."

They went on that way for a while. I had lost touch with the conversation. It seemed obvious that Bernie was trying to lead Reilly somewhere, but I didn't know where and I wouldn't have recognized it if he had succeeded. When I began listening in earnest again, they were talking about Louise.

"Your mother's taking her vacation, I hear," Bernie said.

"Day after tomorrow. She's going up to Tahoe."

"Yon going too?"

"Me? You know me better than that, Bernie. I got to keep busy, writing crap that nobody will buy."

"Look, why don't you get off that weirdo kick, Gar, and write a simple love story—a boy and a girl and a problem."

"Sure," Reilly said heavily, "and a dog and a doctor."

"Why not?"

"Because I don't know anything about that stuff."

"Well, *steal* it for Christ's sake!"

"Oh, stop it. Don't make such a thing. If you don't like the lousy script, say so."

"I haven't read it yet."

"Then give it back to me!"

"I'll ask Julie for it tonight."

Reilly heaved himself onto his crutches and started away. He went out of sight, but I could still hear him.

"No, don't give it back to me," he said quietly. "Read it when you get around to it. Try to get Julie to read it, huh? It's not a bad idea. I need a sale."

"Who doesn't?"

"If I could get to Julie—"

"You can get to Julie any time."

"All right. The last three times, you know what Julie told me? Take it up with Bernie."

"So you took it up with me."

"Goose him a little, huh, Bernie?"

"You know better than that."

"All right. Whatever you can do."

"So long, Gar."

Bernie didn't get up. I heard the door open and close and watched through the crack in the drapes as Reilly swung away down the walk to the hedge and out of sight. His car came to life, and then the sound of another, a sports car, came in over it. Reilly got away with a squeak of tires. The other car roared and stopped. Bernie was in his chair, his hand clenched on his glass.

"You hear it, Mac?" he shouted. "You been listening good? You like to trade jobs—?"

I stayed where I was, listening. Carol Porter was coming down the walk.

The doorbell rang. It rang again. I watched Bernie get up wearily and go to the door.

"Oh, hi, Carol," he said. Then, "All right, Mac, you can come out now!" I went out and the three of us stood around saying hello to one another. Carol had a long white envelope in her hand.

"I hope I'm not interrupting you gentlemen," she said. "What were you yelling about?"

"Philosophy," Bernie said. "I always philosophize at the top of my lungs."

Carol handed him the envelope. "This was in your box. Don't you even pick up your mail anymore?"

Bernie glanced at a small stack of unopened mail on his table and looked at the one Carol had handed him. Then he handed it to me. "Mac's department," he said.

He took off his glasses and rubbed his eyes. "Go ahead, Mac," he said. "Read it out loud."

I was looking at the rubber-stamped address, the blue block letters that read, "Bernie Wolf—" and his street and number. There was no postmark.

There was a stamp, but it hadn't been canceled. I opened it and pulled out a single sheet of paper, as in that first threatening letter. There weren't many words on it. What they said was, "Linda Porter ought to be worth at least twenty thousand dollars. Any day now."

Carol Porter's beautiful red mouth twisted to a scar. She moved toward the brandy bottle, reaching. "Oh, God," she said softly. "Oh, God."

I put the letter back in the envelope and put it in my pocket. I went to the garage, opened it, got the station wagon started and drove away.

* * * *

Bernie followed Carol home that evening and stayed for dinner. We had a few minutes alone to mention the new communication.

"Don't show it to Julie till after the preview," Bernie said. "Give him a break. Hell, it was addressed to me this time. I own it."

"Maybe you'd like to hold it," I said.

"Very funny man," he said, and went away.

Dining dinner, Bernie's attention was devoted almost exclusively to Linda. It paid off; he got to carry her upstairs at bedtime—on his shoulders.

I was sitting in the living room with Carol and Julie when he came down.

"Talk about cradle robbing," Carol said, then clamped her mouth tight.

Julie beamed. Bernie looked at his watch and grinned happily at Julie. "Time to look at the television," he said.

The smile never left Julie's face. "Go ahead. Enjoy yourself. I put a basin of water so you could rest your tired feet while you watch. Don't pay any attention to that little wire attached to the chair."

Bernie considered him thoughtfully. "You just might do it, too," he said.

Julie went on beaming. Bernie went out as Louise Reilly came into the room. Carol was reading a book. Julie was feeling so good he neglected to needle Louise.

"Hi," he said. "Few hands of gin?"

"Thank you, no," Louise said. "I'm trying to get packed."

"Oh. Going somewhere?" Julie said.

From the garage apartment, high, clear and agonized in the still evening air, came a loud, masculine "YIPE!" Julie doubled over in his chair, put his face in his hands and laughed. His big shoulders quivered. The three of us sat and watched him.

"Really," Carol said finally.

Julie looked up, red-faced, gasping. "Electrifying entertainment," he choked.

He collapsed again. Carol returned to her book and Louise waited patiently. I was tingling here and there on Bernie's behalf.

"That's what I want to speak to you about," Louise said.

"Huh?" Julie said, wiping tears from his face.

"About my vacation. Under the circumstances—"

"Oh," Julie said. He leaned toward me with a nudging gesture and spoke behind his hand. "This is the big renunciation scene. She plays this real good."

"With an extra guest in the house," Louise said, and I felt like crawling under my chair, "if you'd prefer that I postpone it—"

Julie's voice was earnest, somber. "It's a matter between you and your conscience, Louise. I wouldn't presume to make the decision for you. I know how much it means."

"It's only that—"

"I understand," Julie said breathily. "Decisions like this arise in everyone's life. I know it isn't easy."

There were a few moments of hushed expectancy. Carol still held her book, but she wasn't reading it. Julie and Louise were gazing at each other, Julie soulfully, Louise quietly glaring. Very gently, Julie said, "I think you ought to go, Louise. You'll be missed, but people have to learn to stand on their own feet. Don't throw your life away in needless sacrifice. Go to Lake Tahoe and throw your money away instead." They continued to stare at each other for about half a minute. Then Julie spread his hands, pleading. "Well, come on!" he shouted. "Feed me a line! Something—anything!"

Slowly Louise rose to her full height. She looked at him for a moment as in the old days she might have looked at a clumsy stagehand. "Very well," she said, and left the room.

Julie got up. "I'll be in the study," he said. "Playtime is over."

When he had gone, Carol looked at me. "Have you shown him the letter yet?" she asked.

"No. Bernie and I decided to wait till after tomorrow."

"Good," she said. "And thanks."

I excused myself and went out to make the rounds. I made them with special care and it took about half an hour. Passing the open window of Julie's study, I glanced in. He was in shirt sleeves, elbows on the desk, reading. The door from the living room opened and Carol looked in.

"I'm going upstairs, Julie. Coming?"

He put down a finger to mark his place. "Got to read the lousy script," he said. "I'll be along, honey."

Carol leaned in the doorway, watching him. After a minute, she turned away and closed the door with a tired, fingering gesture.

I walked on to the front yard and checked everything. I was standing near the drive, looking at the sky, when Bernie came out to his car. He put his thick briefcase on the seat and walked with me down to the front gate. We both looked at the sky.

"Speaking of constellations," he said, "that's some family."

I forget what I said.

"I love them," Bernie said. "Every one, each in his own way. Sophie— she knows the world wouldn't have any problems if everybody could get enough apple strudel. Louise with her grand manner. Carol, taking that nude plunge every morning—sheer defiance. Linda—you have to love Linda, because Linda loves you."

We strolled back to his car.

"Keep your eyes peeled, Mac," he said.

"Good night, Bernie."

He made a face, reached back and scratched himself. "I forgot one," he said. "Julie. Remind me to give the son of a bitch an exploding cigar—after tomorrow."

But the next night there was the business of the tomatoes in the face of Julie's star and the thing in the alley and nobody was thinking about television hot seats or exploding cigars.

CHAPTER SEVEN

That morning after the preview, by the time Linda got up, Julie had left for the studio. It was Saturday and Linda wouldn't be going to school. I had called Walewski because I wanted to show him the new threatening letter and talk it over, and also because Alice planned to be out for a few hours and Carol, too. Louise would be leaving for her vacation and it was Sophie's marketing day. That would leave Linda and me and the big house and I was nervous.

Alice left at about ten o'clock. At eleven, Louise came down with an overnight bag and Gar Reilly was waiting for her in his car. She would drive it to Lake Tahoe.

Around noon, Carol came down, dressed for the street. "I have a luncheon date and a beauty appointment," she said. "I don't know when I'll be back. Is everything all right?"

"Everything's fine," I said.

She glanced out toward the swimming pool, where Walewski and Linda were fishing with homemade bamboo rods trailing kitchen string.

"Be sure to let me know if they catch anything," Carol said, "before tomorrow morning."

We looked at each other and she looked away.

"Sure," I said. "Have a good day."

I watched her leave the house, taut and sleek, her body swaying with that complex touch-me-not provocativeness that I don't know how they learn to do it.

At about twelve-thirty, Sophie served lunch to Linda, Walewski and me and then left for the afternoon. She would return with a taxi-load of raw materials, gathered at obscure markets and fish houses, from which in the next week she would prepare meals that if they were to be offered for public sale, the restaurant owners' association would have to suppress them in order to stay in business. Walewski had a dreamy look in his eyes as she bustled out of the house to the waiting cab. He patted his slight paunch with wistful satisfaction.

"I wonder," he said, "if she could be eased out of here so she could take care of a man that really needs her?"

"If the proposition was decent," I said, "it just might be possible."

"Remind me to mention it."

Linda sat on the middle of her spine on a sofa, looking from one to the other of us.

"What are you talking about?" she said.

"About what a good cook Sophie is," I said.

She thought that over. "Aren't you supposed to be writing a picture?" she said.

As far as she knew, that was what Walewski and I were supposed to be doing.

"Yes," I said, "but it's Saturday."

"My father works on Saturday," she said.

"So he does. You won't tell on us, will you?"

"I might," she said.

"The truth is," I said, "we're stuck."

It was the literal truth. Linda was the last girl in the world to sit in her room and play with dolls as long as there were a couple of adult male "writers" around. Walewski and I hadn't had a chance to discuss the letter and I had been hoping against hope that Linda would take a nap after lunch.

"Tell you what," I said, "if you go up and get dressed, I'll take you down to the ice-cream parlor."

"Okay," she said.

She ran up the stairs, skinning out of her sun suit as she went.

I showed Walewski the letter. He held it carefully by the edges, read it, laid it gently on the floor between his feet and scowled at it.

"You can't do nothing with one of these without a lab," he said.

"Julie won't call in the cops."

"Well, if anything happens, they'll sure as hell call on him."

"I know it."

"This one wasn't even mailed," he complained. "You couldn't even trace it to a substation."

"It got into Bernie Wolf's mailbox."

I told him about the people who had called on Bernie the day before.

"Porter's wife," he said, musing. "Is she fooling around—?"

"That doesn't get us anywhere," I said.

"Excuse me," he said.

"The way Julie wants to do it," I said, "there's only one way. We wait till whoever it is makes a move."

"You think anybody's going to?"

"I don't have the slightest idea."

He picked up the letter, folded it and put it in his pocket. "I'll think on it," he said.

"Catch a nap," I said. "Maybe your unconscious will figure it out."

"I don't believe that crap," he said.

"All right," I said.

Linda came downstairs. I found the keys to the station wagon and we drove down to the ice-cream parlor. We were there for quite a while. On the way home, she fell asleep.

When I carried her up to her room, Walewski was lying on a sofa with his arm over his face. Alice Rummel was pacing the upstairs hall, practically wringing her hands. She calmed enough to open the door and I left her to undress Linda and put her to bed. A couple of minutes passed and she knocked on my bedroom door. She came in, pale and tense.

"I almost lost my mind," she said. "I got home, Linda was gone, you were gone—and he—" she jerked her prim head—"was asleep."

"You sleep when you can," I said. "Linda was with me, he had no problem. I'm sorry if you worried."

"But he was asleep! Anybody could have come in. I could have—"

"No, you couldn't," I said. "He heard you come in, he knew exactly where you were every minute. You couldn't have batted your eyes without letting him know it."

"He was *snoring*!"

I smiled at her. "Did you tiptoe over there to check up on him?"

She blushed, swallowed and turned away. "Yes," she said.

"He didn't want to embarrass you by waking up in your face. Haven't you ever played possum?"

"I'm sorry," she said. "I guess I'm just upset."

"It's all right. It's just between the two of us."

She walked to the window and looked out. "It's very warm."

I agreed. "Good day for a swim," I said.

"I was just thinking the same thing."

"Suppose we meet by the pool. Last one in?"

"Let's!" Then that blush again. "Oh, but I didn't mean—" So she was not without artfulness.

At poolside, she appeared in a two-piece swimsuit that was obviously fresh out of the box. It didn't fit too well, but that could have been the newness. Also, she probably wasn't easy to fit, being, to put it politely, of an excessive slenderness. Both halter and trunks were on the loose side, and her exposed portions were pale compared with Carol's sleek tan.

I managed to refrain from gawking at her and that seemed to help. We raced each other the length of the pool and back and she won. So that was all right. Maybe Walewski's fatherly, unobtrusive presence gave her a feeling of security. Anyway, she appeared, in her quiet way, to be enjoying herself.

Then the telephone rang. There was an instrument in a box on the outside wall of the house and Alice tripped gaily around the pool to answer it.

When she came away, she left the mouthpiece dangling. She returned to her chaise, looked at me stonily and said, "It's for you. It's Carol."

I went to the phone. Carol's voice sounded remote, or it may have been that she was talking with her teeth clenched. "Mac, is Walewski there?"

"Yes," I said.

"Listen, will you please come over to Bernie's right away?"

"Well, sure—"

"Please hurry!"

"All right."

She hung up. I went back to the end of the pool and picked up my towel. "Will you excuse me, please?" I said. "There seems to be something urgent."

"Of course," Alice said.

She flopped onto her stomach with a ladylike flounce. The fire—not exactly a white-hot flame to begin with—had gone out.

It took me about six minutes to shower and dress. Coming downstairs, I ran into Walewski.

"Something up," I said. "Stick around, huh?"

"What else?" he said.

* * * *

Carol's red sports car was parked in front of Bernie's secluded house. I went quickly up the walk and knocked lightly at the door. From inside, she said, "Come in."

She was standing against the wall just inside the door. Her hands were clenched on the curving strap of a large white handbag. Her face was blank and there were white lines, like chalk lines, around the edges of her carefully applied make-up.

Bernie was in his big leather chair. He leaned awkwardly to one side and his right arm dangled over the chair arm. His glasses were askew on his face, so that only his left eye was covered. His right eye showed brown and white above the twisted rim of the lens. The eye was oddly shaped and sightless. There was blood on the right side of his face and an ugly blotch on his temple at the brown hairline. In his dangling right hand was a Luger automatic pistol.

"Was he like this when you came?" I asked.

She nodded stiffly, her head banging lightly against the wall.

"Have you called anyone else?"

She shook her head. It disarranged her blond hair, pushing it up in back.

"Have you been here long?"

She shook her head again. I went over and squatted down and looked at the gun in his hand. He held it so loosely that I could have blown it out of his grip with my own breath.

I straightened up and looked over him at the telephone stand beside the chair. There was an open drawer about four inches deep. It contained a few papers. There was nothing in the six or eight inches of space toward the front.

When I turned to her again, Carol hadn't moved. I looked at her for a few seconds and her hands opened and closed spasmodically. The white purse fell heavily to the floor. She didn't move. I crossed the room, but as I bent to pick up the purse, she leaned down suddenly, pushed me away and picked it up. There were faint blue smudges on the immaculate white of the laminated surface. She put her hand to her face and when it came away there was a smudge on her cheek. I looked at the blue gun in Bernie's flaccid hand.

"Do you know anything about the gun?" I asked her.

"It's Bernie's—I think. He kept it in the drawer. It's a Luger. Bernie got it off a Nazi officer. Bernie was a sergeant and the Nazi didn't want to surrender to him. He demanded identification. Bernie told him his name—his father's name before it got changed to Wolf. Bernie had just got back from a visit to one of the gas chambers. He told the Nazi his name and then he shot him. He shot him six times. He told me about it. He said after the first shot the Nazi started to say something and Bernie shot him in the mouth—"

"Stop it!" I said. "That's enough!"

She clamped her mouth shut and closed her eyes.

"The telephone on the stand," I said. "Is that the one you used to call me?"

She nodded once. There was a muscle pulsating jerkily at one side of her mouth.

"Do you know of any reason why Bernie would shoot himself?"

"No," she said. "He wouldn't."

"I don't know," I said, "but he didn't."

She opened her eyes and looked at me. "I knew—" she said so I could barely make it out, "I knew—you would know—what to do—"

"Was Bernie expecting you?" I asked.

"No," she said. "I just—dropped in."

"After the beauty appointment?"

"Yes."

"Are you getting back on your feet now?" I asked.

"Yes. I think so."

"Have you touched anything in here besides the telephone?"

She turned her head slowly and her eyes slanted down over the door.

"The telephone and the doorknobs. Is that all?"

"Yes," she said.

Her throat was moving convulsively.

"Carol, tell me the exact truth."

"All right."

"Did you shoot Bernie?"

"No."

"And you haven't touched anything except the door and the phone?"

"No. That's all."

I looked at her hands.

"You were wearing gloves when you left the house," I said. "White gloves."

"They're in my purse," she said.

"Were you wearing them when you used the phone, or when you opened the door?"

"No."

"All right, Carol, now listen carefully," I said. "I'm employed by your husband. That makes you a sort of client too. I'm going to try to fix things here so nobody will know you came in. Do you know what that means?"

She nodded.

"Then I'll take you home and call Julie. After that, the police will come around. If you want to tell them you were here, it will be up to you. I'll back you up if you tell them. I will back you up if you don't, too, but my advice would be to tell them."

There was a ten-second pause. Then she said, "All right, Mac."

I went to work on the telephone, carefully keeping the connection button depressed so that if anyone should call, he would get a no-answer and not a busy signal.

"Was the drawer open here when you came in?"

She blinked at the telephone stand. "Yes," she said.

"You didn't touch it or go through it?"

She shook her head against the wall.

I finished with the phone and laid the back of my hand against Bernie's neck on the uninjured side. It wasn't cold. I could feel the stubble of his heavy beard like dull pins.

I went to the door and cleaned the knobs and the door edge where she might have touched it or grabbed it when she first saw him.

"Was the door unlocked?" I asked.

She hesitated. "No," she said. "I have a key."

"Remember to give it to me," I said. "Not now."

"All right," she said.

I checked the lock, set the night latch. Then I opened the door wide enough to let her out without touching it or the jamb with her hands or clothing.

"Go ahead," I said.

She moved away from the wall, turned, doll-like, and walked outside stiffly. I studied the place on the wall where her head had been and found two blond hairs. I picked them off and stuck them in my pocket. I looked down the wall for traces of her, such as threads of fabric, but found nothing. I went outside and closed the door and made sure it was locked. Then I walked her out to the street.

"Can you drive?" I asked.

"I think so," she said.

"Drive carefully. I'll be right behind you."

She got into the little car and made a U-turn on the canyon road. I had to back and fill in Bernie's driveway to get behind her. She drove well and carefully all the way home.

I held her arm to the front door, then turned her, forcing her to look at me.

"Is there any reason you don't want Julie to know you were over there?" I asked.

She met my eyes. "Yes," she said.

"You know what you're asking me to do?"

"I think so."

"Do you think your reason is good enough?"

"Yes."

I opened the door and released her. She stepped inside and looked around at the big room. She swallowed three times in rapid succession. "I'll be in my room," she said, moving away. "Being sick."

I went back to the station wagon and drove as fast as I thought I could get away with to downtown Beverly Hills. I went into a drugstore and bought a toothbrush and some shaving soap. I was fussy enough about the selection that the man on the counter got a little annoyed and I knew he would remember me at least for a few hours.

I drove back to the house, put the station wagon in the garage and went inside. Walewski wandered in from the breakfast room.

"Stay here a minute, huh?" I said.

He nodded and glanced curiously up the stairs. I went into Julie's study and dialed the studio. It took them a while to reach him.

"Are you on a safe phone?" I asked.

"What—? I don't know. What's up?"

"Nothing to do with Linda," I said. "Find a phone and call me back."

"This one's all right. Nobody else on it."

I told him Bernie was dead. There was a long silence. "No," he said quietly. "It can't be."

"I'm sorry," I said. "It's true."

"Mac—"

"Somebody will have to call the police. Do you want me to do it?"

"I don't—no, stay out of it. Did you find him?"

"Yes. I happened to go over there. Walewski was at the house."

"It can't be—Mac—"

"I'll have to call the police, Julie."

"No. You have to stay out of it. You got other things to do. I'll call."

"It won't make sense if you call from the studio."

"I'll go over there—"

"I'll be glad to do it—"

"No!" He was firmer now. "I don't want you to do it."

"All you would have to do would be to go to that neighborhood some-where. But it would work out better if you used Bernie's phone."

"Yeah—yeah, all right."

"If you go in, walk very carefully and don't touch him. Most of all, absolutely don't touch Bernie, or do anything that will jar the gun out of his hand."

"The gun—his hand—no, I can't believe it—"

"Then, Julie, I guess you'll have to see for yourself. I wish I could change it."

"All right, Mac," he said finally. "I'll go. Then I'll call the cops."

Walewski was wandering around the living room. He looked at me with the old shrewd look.

"You wouldn't want me to tell you what happened," I said. "It will be in the papers pretty soon."

"What do you want me to do?" he said.

"Go somewhere, not too far, and check in so I can call you when I need you."

"Whatever you say, Mac."

"It's just that I want you to be a free agent."

He nodded, picked up his hat and left.

Out by the pool, Alice was lying on her back on one of the chaises with a set of blinders on her eyes. I sat down next to her. She roused slowly, re-moved the blinders and blinked at me.

I told her about Bernie. She stared at me, shaking her head. Then she began to cry silently. I took one of her hands. It was cold and limp.

"Will you do something for me?" I asked.

"If I can." Her blue eyes cleared.

"If anyone should ask you," I said, "I want you to forget about that tele-phone call from Carol."

"Forget—? But Mr. Walewski knew—"

"I've already taken care of Walewski. Will you do this for me?"

She withdrew her hand slowly. "If it's important to you—"

"It's important to several people."

"All right," she said.

"Thanks," I said.

I went back inside and wandered around and waited for Julie and the cops.

CHAPTER EIGHT

There were two of them; a big guy named Holland, a lieutenant; and a thin, gangling sergeant with a game leg. They showed up about six o'clock and we sat in Julie's study. Julie had wanted me to stay out of sight altogether, but I explained that I would have to be in on it so I would know how to defend myself if it should come to that. Julie saw the point. He was badly shaken, his big face was drained and gray, and he sat slumped in his chair, glum-lipped and uncooperative.

Lieutenant Holland was a man with a heavy, closed face and a way of coming at you from different directions. Soft-spoken and offhand, he gave the simultaneous impression of friendly acceptance and stubborn disbelief.

"You say, Mr. Porter, that you went over to Wolf's house and the door was locked—"

"I have a key to Bernie's house. He has a key to this house. We're back and forth."

"I see. What time was this, Mr. Porter?"

Julie told them.

"You wouldn't ordinarily go out of your way like that, would you? I thought Wolf worked for you."

"Sure I would, if I wanted to talk privately. Today I was on the way home from the studio, so I wanted to see him, I dropped off."

"How come Mr. Wolf wasn't at the studio?"

"He doesn't come in on Saturday except for something special."

"Do you always work Saturdays?"

"Not always. Today I did."

"What were you working on?"

"What was I—? For Christ's sake, what does a producer work on?"

"If you don't mind," Holland said gently, "a man is dead."

"All right!" Julie slammed Iris hand on the desk. "You go ahead—you ask me any stinking questions you want to. I'll do my best. Just make sense to me, that's all."

"I'll try, Mr. Porter."

As if to switch the mood, the gimpy sergeant wandered over and sat down near me.

"Who are you?" he said. "I forget."

"I'm working on a picture with Mr. Porter," I said.

"What kind of a picture?"

"A crime picture."

"You a writer?"

"No. I'm a technical adviser."

"Oh." There was a hard gleam in his eye. "You a criminal?"

"No."

"Lay off him!" Julie said. "He knows nothing about it. I found Bernie."

Lieutenant Holland sighed. "So you unlocked the door and went in," he said, "and there was Mr. Wolf—dead."

"Yeah."

"What was your first thought, Mr. Porter?"

"First thought? I guess—I was thinking Bernie shot himself. What else could I think. He had a gun in his hand—"

"Did you look at him closely?"

"No. I just picked up the phone and called the cops—the police."

"That's all right," the sergeant said. "I don't mind being called a cop."

"Do you know of any enemies Wolf had, Mr. Porter?"

"Enemies? Bernie? What the hell—well, in our business, some people like you, some don't. But if you mean mortal enemies—no."

His eyes shifted for a moment and met mine. I looked away. "Understand, Mr. Porter," Holland said, "we have to get all the information we can."

"Okay," Julie said. "Go ahead. Let's get it done."

There were some more questions, about Bernie's habits and associates, what kind of work he did and so on. The sergeant wrote down a list of names. I wished him well with them.

He must have guessed I was thinking about him, because when Holland ran out of questions, the gimpy one confronted me again.

"You got any identification, Mac?"

I looked at Julie, who shrugged slightly.

"Sure," I said.

I handed the sergeant my ID card. He raised his eyebrows, passed it to Holland, who passed it back to me.

"That's a private eye picture you're making, Mr. Porter?" Gimpy said.

"Sort of," Julie said.

"How's it coming?"

"All right," Julie said.

"Did you know Mr. Wolf?" Holland asked me.

"A little."

"Did you see him today?"

"No," I said.

"Where are you staying while you're in California?" Gimpy asked.

"I'm living here," I said.

"Oh, right here with Mr. Porter."

"Uh-huh."

"For how long?"

I spread my hands. "Can't tell for certain. Not long."

"What's your professional opinion of this picture Mr. Porter is making?"

"I'm not sure I'm making it," Julie cut in. "We're working on a script. If it turns out—"

"Oh. Just working on it."

"What would be your professional opinion on Bernie Wolf's case?" Holland asked. "Do you think he shot himself?"

"All I know," I said, "is what Mr. Porter told me. I couldn't say.

"You didn't see the body then?"

"No."

"You've been here in the house all day?"

"I went out a couple of times."

"When?" That one came like an arrow.

"Around one-thirty I took Linda Porter to the ice-cream parlor. Then about three-forty-five I drove downtown for a few minutes."

"What for?"

"For a change of scene mostly. I had to get a couple of things, personal things."

"What kind of things?"

"A toothbrush for one and some shaving soap."

"What store did you go to?"

"A drugstore at Santa Monica and Roxbury."

"What the hell you getting at?" Julie said. "You think he shot Bernie?"

Both Holland and Gimpy looked at Julie. But it was a different look than the one they'd given me. Julie was getting the big-producer-kid-gloves treatment all the way.

"We didn't say anybody shot Bernie," Holland said, "except Bernie himself."

"You sure have been implying it," Julie said. It was the fastest recovery I had ever seen in my life, and it took them in. Gimpy looked at his notepad and Holland shifted his hat.

"We have to cover every possible angle," he said. "The fact is, Bernie Wolf was murdered."

Julie rose from his chair and leaned on his fists, looking across it. "I'm glad you finally got around to coming out with it," Julie said. "Here's the way I feel about it. You find out who did it, it's a thousand bucks apiece to each of you, from me personally."

Holland got up slowly and put on his hat. Gimpy limped to the study door.

"Oh, we'll find out, Mr. Porter," Holland said. "But save your money. We're public servants and you're a taxpayer."

Julie shrugged. "Okay. Do it your way. If I can help, let me know."

"We'll do that," Gimpy said, and opened the door.

Beyond him in the living room, Carol Porter had come to the bottom of the stairway and was standing like a tree, watching the study door. Julie sank into his chair. I followed Holland and Gimpy out there. Holland wiggled his hat.

"Mrs. Porter?" he said.

Carol nodded.

"We're police, Mrs. Porter; I guess you've heard about Bernie Wolf."

"Yes."

"I imagine you're pretty upset—"

"I am. Bernie was a dear friend of the family."

"Well, this gentleman here—" he waved in my direction—"tells us he was here around the house most of the day. I wonder if you could substantiate that for me." Carol stared at him coldly. "Just so we can tie this up," he said.

Carol looked at me and at Holland and then beyond us. I turned and Julie was in the doorway of his study, listening, brooding at the backs of the two policemen.

"I couldn't say," Carol said finally. "I was out most of the day myself."

I glanced up the stairs and Alice was standing in the hall outside Linda's room, looking down at us.

"Oh," Holland said to Carol. "You were out shopping and so forth?"

"Mostly and so forth," Carol said. "I had a beauty appointment at one o'clock. I left the beauty parlor at about three-fifteen and did a little window shopping. I came home about four o'clock. Mac—this gentleman—was here when I left and when I got back."

Gimpy made a couple of notes. Holland looked up the stairs and around at me and then at Julie and nodded. He started to put his hat on, changed his mind and carried it to the door. Gimpy followed him with a friendly wave.

"We'll probably want to talk to you again, Mr. Porter," Holland said.

Julie just nodded. The two of them went outside. We stood where we were until we heard their car going away down the drive. Then Alice turned around and went into Linda's room. Carol came on down the stairs and went to the bar. Julie went into his study and closed the door. I went out to the swimming pool and lay down on a chaise and looked at the blue, blue sky.

CHAPTER NINE

The household relaxed slowly after Holland and Gimpy left. Gloom and grief remained, but the tension eased, especially for Carol. And for Linda's sake, through the next two days, everyone made an effort to be jaunty when possible.

At around three in the afternoon on the day before Linda's birthday, a telegram came from Louise Reilly at Lake Tahoe.

"JUST HEARD TRAGIC NEWS OF BERNIE'S DEATH," it read. "SHALL I FLY HOME?"

Julie drafted a one-word reply: "NO," which Carol rewrote as: "ALL IS WELL, DARLING; PLEASE STAY AND REST. LOVE, CAROL, JULIE AND LINDA."

I was aware of grief in Julie, but as master of the house, he was either unable or unwilling to acknowledge it in himself. Only for a moment he let down, as if he felt secure in the presence of an outsider. He looked at me with shadowed eyes across his massive desk.

"He was my boy, Mac!" he said. "Not like a son—a son isn't that close. Bernie was—" he thrust his arm out, his hand open—"my arm! Part of my brain! Maybe the best part. Maybe this washes me up."

"Not you," I said. "Plenty of one-armed men come back strong."

"It wasn't just me alone. Everybody—around the studio, in the family—Bernie was a special person. Sophie, Linda, Louise—even Carol."

"Bernie felt the same," I said. "He told me."

That was the end of it from Julie to me. He had gone to great pains to keep the news from Linda until after her birthday party, and apparently with success.

* * * *

The party turned out to be a hilarious affair, on which Julie and I spied shamelessly until driven out of the breakfast room by our own mirth. We wound up at poolside, where we flopped on a couple of chaises and gradually quieted. Julie fell asleep. I took a turn around the pool. Occasional shouts came from inside the house. I caught sight of Sophie, very busy in the kitchen, and Carol and Alice coming and going, and guessed they were serving the refreshments. That could account for the peaceful atmosphere. I wandered back to the lounging end of the pool, lay back on the chaise next to Julie and covered my eyes with my arm.

Figuring it out later, I decided it must have happened at about that moment, inside the house, but neither Julie nor I had any advance warning. I heard the breakfast-room door and glanced that way.

"Here comes Linda," I said.

Julie sat up, the chaise squeaking under his big frame. Linda came on slowly, one hand hovering near her face. Her long, black hair was rumpled. There were some ice-cream stains on her frilly party dress and the strap on one of her patent leather slippers was broken.

"Hi, Linda," I said.

She ignored me and went to Julie, he reached for her, then hesitated when she looked up at him.

"Is it true?" she asked. "About Bernie? Is Bernie dead?"

Julie's eyes flashed to mine and I shook my head. "Who said so?" Julie asked her.

"Roger. He said Bernie was dead and everybody was talking about it."

Julie held out his arms.

"Is he?" she asked. "Is Bernie dead?"

"Yes, baby," Julie said. "I was going to tell you right after your birthday."

"Why? Why is he dead?"

Julie lifted her onto his knees. "Look, honey," he said, "will you let me tell you about it after the party?"

"But—why?" she said. "Won't I ever see Bernie again?"

"Maybe someday," Julie said.

By some insight peculiar to children, she knew it was useless to push the question further. If she cried, I couldn't tell, and there was no sign later. Pretty soon Julie held her away, kissed her, straightened her hair and set her on her feet. "Better take charge of your party, huh?" he said.

"All right," she said. "Goodbye. Goodbye, Mac."

"Goodbye," I said.

She left us and walked away to the house and inside. Julie and I sat there and looked at various bits of nothing.

* * * *

By the middle of the next day, everyone was edgy again. Julie had come home from the studio at two-thirty in the afternoon to find another telegram from Louise Reilly. I was passing the open study when I heard an explosive curse and glanced in. He waved a paper at me.

"Money she needs!" he said. "Against her next wages. I ought to charge her a hundred percent; teach her a lesson. You know what that fool woman does?"

"I guess not," I said.

"She goes up to Tahoe, gets a place on the California side, all real re-spectable. Then she sneaks around to Nevada every night and leaves her money. How she gets home after I don't know. Maybe the casino stakes her to a taxi. It would be money in their pockets."

I had not pictured Louise as a compulsive gambler and the idea was novel. I tried to imagine her, regal, self-possessed, with that carriage, that poise, bending over a crowded crap table or studying the revolutions of a roulette wheel, but I couldn't. She didn't fit.

Julie was dialing the phone. "I had to quit playing gin with her," he said. "It cost me money to win!" Then to the phone, "Hello—? Listen, honey, wire a hundred bucks to Louise Reilly at Tahoe. You've got the address somewhere—read it to me—yeah, that's it. Anything new?…"

I crossed the living room and Carol came out of the kitchen and went into the study. A few minutes later sounds came through the closed door, voices were rising. For the second time that day, Carol and Julie were in a sharp exchange. I put it down to frayed nerves and went upstairs out of earshot.

CHAPTER TEN

The combination of the party and her grief over Bernie had kept Linda in her room all day. Alice stayed with her and because I wanted to keep clear of the feuding downstairs, I arranged for room service for the three of us, bringing dinner up on a tray. We ate together in Linda's room, but there wasn't any conversation.

Julie had an appointment for the evening and I knew that Garwood Reilly had called on him just before dinner. I could hear Julie shouting at Reilly, but had no idea what it was about. I sat around and tried to cheer Linda up and didn't get anywhere and wished I could justify a call to Walewski. We might, I thought, at least sit around and chin.

At about nine-thirty I went out to make the rounds and when I came in, Carol was alone in the living room, wearing a blouse and slacks, lying on one of the long sofas with her feet up, reading the papers and eating an apple.

"All secure for the night, Captain?" she said.

"One can never be sure," I said. "We hope for the best."

It was natural, following the events of the past few days, that the threat to Linda had become remote, even a little ridiculous, but Carol had never ridden me in quite this way.

"How about having a chink and a little chat?" she said.

"I don't mind."

She waved with the apple. "You know where everything is," she said. "I'd like a stinger."

The newspapers rattled behind me as I went to the bar and looked for the ingredients.

"They aren't getting ahead very fast on the Bernie Wolf case, are they?" she said.

"They don't have much to go on."

"I should think they'd be questioning everyone Bernie ever knew. You know—really digging."

"They don't always give everything to the papers. And then sometimes the papers don't want to use names when there's nothing definite."

I made her a sort of a stinger and poured myself a slug of bourbon.

"What's your theory on the case?" she asked.

"I don't have any," I said.

"Oh, come on," she said. "You must be thinking about it."

"I think about it, but I don't get out much."

"You were a cop once, weren't you?"

"Yes, I was a cop, in Chicago."

"Did you ever work on any murder cases? Or what do they call it—homicides?"

"A few."

"Well, what was it like? I mean, what did you do?"

"Mostly leg work and hanging around talking and listening. Nothing glamorous ever happened."

"Is that why you got out of it?"

"No, I was bounced."

"Oh. Why, if it's any of my business?"

"I call it politics. Some might have other explanations. It was quite a long time ago."

She had finished her stinger and held out the empty glass. I took it to the bar and started a fresh one.

"Well," she said, "take this thing with Bernie. As a cop, how would you go about solving it, if you could get out?"

"If I was a cop, I'd probably be doing just what you suggested; checking out Bernie's friends and associates."

"Looking for a cast-off mistress maybe?"

"Maybe," I said.

"Or it might have been robbery."

"It might—except that it's unlikely a robber would put the gun in Bernie's hand and it's even more unlikely that Bernie would have been sitting down at the time."

"I didn't think of that."

"It might have been an accident," I said.

"Accident? How?"

"Well, some friend of Bernie's might have dropped in and they got to talking about, say, guns. Bernie or the friend would take the gun out and they might be fooling with it and it might go off."

"But in that case, whoever it was would tell the police. If he was a friend of Bernie's, he'd report it for goodness' sake!"

I looked at her. "Would you?" I said.

She returned my look for a minute. "The reason I didn't want anybody to know I had been there didn't have anything to do with shooting Bernie," she said. "I don't know whether I would or not."

I tasted some more of the bourbon.

"Would you like to talk a little about why you didn't want to be found with Bernie?" I asked.

She shook her head definitely. "No," she said.

"It might be easier now than later."

"I don't think so."

"All right. Did Julie make his appointment?"

"I don't know. He left on time. In a lousy mood."

"Because of Reilly?"

"I guess so. He always gets so steamed—Julie I mean. I guess he has a guilt complex about Reilly. But he can't buy everything Reilly dreams up. The guy is such a weirdo! Like wanting Bernie's job yet!"

"Reilly wanted Bernie's job?"

"He expected it! They wound up yelling at each other, as usual, and Reilly stamping out on his damn crutches. Julie was shaking. See, Bernie used to handle it for him mostly."

"How did Bernie feel about Reilly?"

"Well, Bernie had a way. He could separate somebody's work from their personality. And then, Bernie didn't have any guilt feelings about Reilly. In fact it was maybe the other way around."

"How so?"

"Well, for one thing, Reilly is kind of anti-Semitic, in a sneaky way. One of these 'some of my best friends' types. You know?"

"Uh-huh."

"I don't know how much it bothered Bernie personally. It didn't show. But I heard him try to reason with him. He said Reilly should know better."

"But Reilly never learned?"

"No. Even Mama couldn't seem to get it over to him."

"About Mrs. Reilly—Louise. Does Julie feel guilty about her too?"

"I don't know. He shouldn't. She's a good housekeeper and worth her pay. And she was a good actress, awfully good. Except in pictures. She just couldn't. She had every chance in the world and Julie made most of them for her. She had a kind of a block. And she had a bad attitude, maybe for the same reason. She got the idea she was above the movies. Only the stage was honest work. The trouble was, it got so there just wasn't any work on the stage, honest or not. Maybe once in a while. So she couldn't make it and she invented an excuse. Which is about the same as Reilly being anti-Semitic." I was thinking it over when she said, "Whew, that was quite a speech. How about another drink?"

While I was making them, Alice came downstairs, shy and diffident as a country cousin. Carol greeted her in a friendly way. "Sit down, Alice, have a drink."

Alice would have a glass of sherry. I found some for her.

"Mac was telling me about when he was a policeman," Carol said.

"Oh? I'll bet that was interesting," Alice said.

"Not very," I said.

It went like that. Nobody said anything much. Alice got more and more uncomfortable and that made Carol restless and she started to needle Alice. Finally, as if realizing it, she cut herself off, got up and said she was going to bed. Alice started to get up, too, but Carol waved her down again.

"Stick around," she said. "Get him to tell you the story of his life. It could be great."

She went upstairs. Alice was massaging the stem of her glass nervously. She had the fingers for it—long, slender, pale, very clean looking—except for a faint dark smudge, bluish, on two or three of them. It was a little surprising. Alice was a clean type, not to say pristine.

"I'm sorry if I broke anything up," she said.

"You didn't. More sherry?"

"No, thank you."

I was very depressed. I had got to thinking about Bernie Wolf and was frustrated because I couldn't do anything about him. I had spent most of the day in a closet, so to speak, with Linda and Alice. Now I was frustrated by Alice, who might, I thought, be made into a reasonable playmate, if only I had the inclination and the patience.

Struggling to open the conversation, I came up with the least likely kind of gambit. "That rubber stamp letter Linda found," I said, "that first night. Where did she find it?"

She blinked at me. "It was—outside somewhere. I don't remember clearly. Out by the pool, I think. Why?"

I shrugged. "I don't know exactly. Something's working on me, but not hard enough I guess."

She looked into her glass, twisting it again. "Would you tell me the story of your life?" she said.

"Gladly," I said, "but it would probably put you to sleep and I'd have to carry you upstairs."

"Well," she said, "I'm not very heavy."

We studied our respective drinks. Suddenly I couldn't sit there any longer. It was getting hard to breathe.

"I think I'll take a stroll around the grounds for a last checkup," I said. "Want to come along?"

I was vaguely disappointed when she said yes.

We went out through the breakfast room and around the pool to the gate at the corner of the garage. The moon was up and the back yard was subtly shadowed. There was a high fragrance of orange blossom.

I checked the rear gate, not that it needed checking. As we started back toward the house, the light was up in Carol's room overlooking the pool. She had undressed and was standing, nude, at an open window, smoking a cigarette.

Alice lowered her head and quickened her pace, veering toward the garage. In the shadow of its wall, we could no longer see the upstairs windows. Alice was taut as a fiddle string. When she spoke, in a kind of muted growl, she sounded breathless and desperate.

"I guess I just never will understand," she said.

"Maybe you try too hard."

"What?"

"Carol had no way to know we were out here. And she can't be seen from the street."

I hadn't meant to defend her—or vice versa—but it came out that way. Alice spoke fiercely between her teeth. "She knows you're usually in the breakfast room when she takes that morning plunge—after her husband has left the house." I passed that. After a couple of minutes, she took a long breath and let it out slowly, unevenly. "I'm sorry," she said. "There was no excuse for that. I just work here—the same as you."

She was linking us again. She fascinated and repelled me at once. I didn't know what to do about her, but I had to do something, if only to see what would happen.

What happened was this: I slid my arm around her waist. She stiffened momentarily, then gave in and turned to me. There was an absurdly small amount of her. Our noses bumped awkwardly and she put her hand on my arm with a kind of nervous haste. When I kissed her, her lips were thin and taut against her closed teeth.

After a few seconds I released her. She just stood there. I took her hand and we went through the garage. There was more warmth in the pressure of her hand than there had been in the kiss. I wondered if she considered herself to have been assaulted, then decided not. It was just that she didn't know how and I doubted that I was the one to teach her.

We went down the drive toward the front gate. We passed an open stretch in the chain link fence where vines and climbing roses had recently been cleared away. We went on for eight or ten paces and I stopped her with a light squeeze of my hand. I put my finger to my mouth and gestured to her to stay where she was. She nodded.

I went back along the fence, found a shadow to stand in and looked out at the street for quite a while. When I rejoined Alice, I found that hand-holding time was over, which was just as well.

She declined a nightcap and I went upstairs with her, in a manner of speaking. According to nightly custom, we both went in to check on Linda.

She was all right. Heading for my own room, I bumped into something and Alice jumped to help me catch and right it. For a moment, our faces were close. I kissed her again. She closed her eyes and it was a more interesting kiss than the one behind the garage, but not very. As we straightened, she put her mouth to my ear.

"What was it you were looking at down on the driveway?" she asked.

"Nothing," I whispered. "Don't worry about it."

She seemed to accept that. I moved to the connecting door and she came after me, hurrying.

"Mac—"

"Yeah?"

She had her hands flat against my chest, looking up. Her eyes had depth in the half-dark room.

"Nothing," she said, turning away.

I watched her go away, pausing briefly at the four-poster, and disappear. Then I went to my own room, undressed and got in bed.

I lay there, wondering. There were quite a few things to wonder about, but mainly I wondered whether I should have told Alice the truth—that it had been Lieutenant Holland and his gimpy sergeant partner, sitting out there in their car across the street, smoking and waiting.

If they had cased the place with any shrewdness at all, they could only be waiting for Julie to come home. There was absolutely nothing I could do about it. If I should go out there and they should decide to take me in for a few questions—as was likely—then Linda would be left unwatched.

So I had another fat frustration.

But Pavlov demonstrated, I think, that unbearable frustration puts you to sleep. Anyway, it puts dogs to sleep. And me.

* * * *

I woke to the sound of finger tips at my door. I looked at my watch and it was eleven-thirty. I had been asleep for an hour. I lay still, listening, and the tapping came again. Then the door opened silently.

It was Carol. She came in quickly, closing the door behind her. I got up on my elbows. She crossed the room, trading some diaphanous material. I was sharply aware of her scent.

When she leaned over the bed, I saw that there was nothing under the negligee but a lot of Carol.

"Mac—" She sat down on the edge of the bed and I moved back a little.

"Is Julie home?" I asked her.

"No, listen, I have to talk to you—"

"Not in here."

"Oh, God; listen, Mac. It has to be right now. I'm scared and I have to tell you—"

"I'll be glad to talk about anything," I said. "But not here like this."

"Please, will you listen, Mac."

"Go put something on," I said. "I'll meet you downstairs."

Her hands were fists on the bedclothes beside me. She stared at me for about half a minute, then slid off the bed. Starting up, she stumbled over one of my shoes and fell. I climbed out, grabbed my dressing gown and helped her up. She leaned heavily against me for a moment and I held her while she got her balance.

"All right," she said. "But hurry."

I walked with her to the door, opened it and she started into the hall. Three steps and she froze. I had snapped my light on when the door opened and I froze just behind her, with my dressing gown awry across my shoulders. Julie Porter was standing on the next to the last step, with one hand on the railing.

He looked very tired. His massive shoulders slumped, exaggerating the swell of his paunch. His eyes were darkly shadowed. But he had one advantage over us. He had all his clothes on.

Carol took half a step toward him and stopped.

"Julie—" His mouth moved in his face and he made a small brushing gesture with his free hand. When he spoke, his voice was barely audible, but we could hear it all right. "Get out," he said.

Carol looked at him steadily, adjusting her negligee carefully. "Julie, will you listen to me for a minute—" He shook his head and his jowls quivered. "No," he said hoarsely. "I won't listen. Get out. I'll call you a cab. Send for your things."

Carol's back tightened, her head went up and tilted slightly to one side. She turned quickly and walked away down the hall. Julie and I were looking at each other.

"No use talking, huh, Julie?" I said.

"No," he said. "Send me a bill for your time."

He let go of the railing, turned around and started slowly, heavily, down the stairs.

I went into my room, got out my suitcase and threw stuff into it. Even then, I kept thinking he'd cool off enough so that we could discuss it. I packed and dressed and I had just finished when there was another tapping at my door, the connecting door this time, from Linda's room. I cursed under my breath and opened it.

It was Alice in a nightgown and bathrobe.

"What happened?" she asked. "I heard—"

"Julie just threw me out," I said.

"No—why—?"

"It's the longest short story in the world. I'll write you about it," I said. "I want to look at Linda once."

"Of course," she said, stepping aside.

I went into the small boudoir, leaned over the little four-poster bed and looked at her. She was asleep with her mouth open. Her white teeth showed between her bps. Her black hair was like a giant fan on the pillow under her head.

"So long, doll," I said.

Alice was waiting in the doorway. I pulled the two threatening letters out of my pocket and handed them to her. "Will you give these to Julie when he cools off?" I said.

"Yes," she said. "But, Mac—where will you go?"

"I got a lot of places to go. I'll write you a letter."

Her face was crumpling. I massaged her little chin with my fist.

"Take care of Linda," I said.

She just looked at me. I picked up my suitcase and got out of the room and down the stairs.

Julie was sitting at his desk, staring into space. Outside there was the sound of a car on the drive. That would be the taxi. I stood in the open door-way of the study.

"Do you want me to wait till you can get Walewski up here?" I asked him.

He wouldn't look at me. "No," he said. His voice rose to the familiar roar. For an instant I thought we could straighten it out again. He was back in form. "No," he shouted. "I'm home! I can take care of my own!"

There were quick footsteps behind me. I looked around to see Carol crossing to the door, an overnight bag in her hand, a fur coat over her arm. She didn't look at me nor into the study.

"All right," I said to Julie. "Goodbye."

He didn't say anything. I went to the door and Carol was trying to get it open. I helped her. We went outside and the cab was waiting.

"How about a lift?" I asked her.

"It's all right with me," she said, climbing in.

I got in beside her. "I'll get out as soon as we hit a cabstand," I said.

The driver got it started and we rolled down the drive. Carol was making up her lips.

"I don't really care too much where you go," she said.

So that was all of that. End of assignment. The hard square end of a long nothing, like the thing they use in the butcher shop to pound the gristle out of meat.

Except that after we got through the gates and headed toward Sunset Boulevard, a car eased out from the curb of the side street and drifted onto our tail. I looked back and it was the car I had seen earlier. It still contained Lieutenant Holland and the gimpy one. It came along with us, not too close, not too far back.

I was mildly interested to note that after I left Carol and found a cab to myself, it was me they stayed with. I hadn't meant to do her any favors.

CHAPTER ELEVEN

There wasn't much sense in trying to duck them. They had legitimate claims to any information they could get out of me. Not that it would be pleasant. I was a stranger in town and they could put their boots to me with impunity.

I asked the driver about a downtown hotel and he seemed to think it over.

"Well, what do you want—like the Biltmore, Ambassador, Statler—or what, I mean?"

"Nothing shiny," I said. "A clean place, reasonable."

He mentioned one. "Kind of old," he said. "Okay though. Being practically right on Skid Row, it don't have a fancy trade."

I said that would be fine.

When he pulled up in front and I looked around for the small posse, it was not to be seen. They couldn't have lost us, I drought. But then I thought, headquarters is just around the corner. Maybe they were between shifts.

A smart bellboy took my bag and I paid off the driver and went in to register. The place was, as he had said, old and a little tired-looking. But it was well-run and I felt more at home here in the guts of the city than out along the golden fringes.

My room was on the fifth floor, overlooking the gaudy lights of Skid Row. There was some traffic noise, which I was used to, but inside, the walls were thick and it was quiet. I took off my coat and tie and shoes and lay down on the bed. Pink-gray light filtered through the half-shut slats of the Venetian blinds. There was an armchair near the window and it looked awfully empty.

I felt very bad about me—a poor, hard-working, right-minded bird dog, misunderstood, friendless in a strange town, kicked around for something I didn't even do; underpaid—why, compared with that loud-talking, mixed-up Hollywood crowd, I was a paragon...

And so on for some time. The trouble with it was, not only did it undermine my morale, it kept me awake and caused a burning in my stomach. I had a mental chat with myself as to the relative good sense in sending down for a bottle of medicine as opposed to going out for a glass of milk.

The shade of a gaunt cow wandered in and sat in the armchair, displaying a swollen udder.

Somebody has to drink up that surplus milk, I decided.

* * * *

It was after midnight and the hotel dining room was closed. The clerk mentioned a short order restaurant down the street.

The hotel block was dark and quiet, but in the next was the beginning of a long double row of honky-tonks. Both streets and sidewalks were busy. I crossed one street, with some difficulty, then crossed again and made for the restaurant in the next block.

As I reached it, a black car with a noticeable radio antenna slid to a smooth stop at the curb. From the cafe door I glanced back. The rear door swung open and there, with one foot planted on the curb, was my new friend, Lieutenant Holland.

I stood there. The Lieutenant took a spit for himself in the gutter.

"Go ahead," he said. "Have your coffee."

"Join me?" I said.

He shook his head. "We'll wait," he said.

I could see Gimpy beside him in back, and they had a uniformed driver. None of them looked like monsters. All that would be required would be that I should talk frankly and not hold anything out. And I could have my coffee first. It assumed sudden importance that I was already one up on the Lieutenant—that I was going to have milk instead of coffee—stubbornly, willfully, deceptively—and enjoy it. But once inside the warm, grease-laden atmosphere of the cafe, I felt my hands shaking.

In a booth in a far corner was a mixed quartet of young Mexicans, dressed for a date, giggling and talking disc-jockey American. There was an old codger at the counter, snoozing over a cup of coffee from which no steam rose. There was a burly, competent-looking waitress and there was me. I ordered apple pie and milk and fell to in a lackadaisical way, dawdling over it, playing for nonexistent time. The sour-bland aftertaste of the milk was irritating. I felt thick-tongued. It would make it hard to talk when talking time came.

And what else would make it hard?

Julie Porter had fired me. What did I owe him? Carol had been the sole, only, exclusive cause of the firing. So what did I owe her? It was entirely possible that she had killed Bernie Wolf. Mechanically possible; I mean, it could fit together all right. Only Carol didn't have much motive. She loved Bernie. Even if he had been trying to break it off, she had too many other things going for her to risk a thing like murder. Carol was basically healthy.

Besides, she had that alibi at the beauty parlor and I had personally checked it out.

As for Julie, I would be fully paid for my time and effort to date. It could be said that we were quits, that from the moment of termination of our contract, I was as free of obligation to Julie as he was of me. Logical, but impracticable.

Under such a system, no attorney would be a reliable agent in confidence. I didn't have anything like the social or legal standing of an attorney, but I had to go by the same rules, including that if Julie had killed Bernie and I knew it, I would have to persuade him to turn himself in for it and, if subpoenaed, I would have to testify to my own knowledge, as to facts.

There weren't any facts, but there was some very touchy speculation. Like—what would you do, I wondered, if your beloved and trusted "right hand" was fooling around with your wife? If you were Julie Porter, I mean, with a temper like that? After you had lost so badly before? How would you react in the sudden, blinding moment of discovery?

But there were no facts—that I knew of. I would be unable to talk frankly to Lieutenant Holland and I doubted that he would be understanding about it. I tried—and by far from the first time in my career (because every person and every situation is different from all the others)—to pinpoint my reason; to frame a precise, convincing explanation that would go down with Holland. But I couldn't. It was more than a feeling and less than a formula. So it wasn't much good to anyone but me, and it was all I had.

I ordered another glass of milk, hoping the Lieutenant would notice what a cool one I could be, and sipped at it. The Mexican kids got up to leave. They were gay and giggling as they passed behind me. Then as they reached the cash register near the front window, silence fell around them like a curtain. The sudden banging of the cash register was an explosion.

"Hey," one of the boys said, very low, "those cops out there!"

And the other, "What're they, just sittin'?" One of the girls muttered something and the other laughed.

"I didn't do nothin'," the first boy said, "you do anything?"

"Hell no, I didn't—I was just walkin' along doin' nothin'—" Because all this was obviously true, they were happy again and milled out of the place with a touch of swagger, the girls' buttocks twitching defiantly.

Lieutenant Holland and Gimpy got out of the car as I emerged from the cafe. A sodden, bewhiskered citizen shambled out of a doorway, clearing his throat to put the bite on me, caught sight of the law and stopped dead. I walked over to the car and Holland and Gimpy flanked me quietly.

"Empty your pockets on top of the car," Holland said.

I stared at him.

"Come on!" he said.

I did it. There wasn't much.

"The whole bit?" I said.

Holland nodded. I put my hands flat on the car top and they frisked me carefully. Behind me, the old boy with the whiskers made a high sound in his throat.

"Looky there—" he muttered, "fella walk right out of a joint and get himself tapped... Can't even buy a cup coffee on the street no more..."

"All right," Holland said. "Pick up your stuff."

I was gathering it up, having a little trouble snagging the loose coins on the slick car top, when the *paisano* shambled up, looking anxious and indignant.

"Hey, pal—buddy—" he said, as if we were alone, "you want me to call a lawyer, somethin'? If you got a dime for the call... Write a letter to Matt Weinstock—?"

"Who?" I said.

"Weinstock—colyumist—you know—" I found a dime and flipped it to him.

"Sure, thanks," I said.

He caught the coin, worked his mouth and Gimpy gave him a light shove.

"Get moving," he said.

The old boy moved on reluctantly. The trouble I was in, I should have been good for more than a dime.

Gimpy got in the back seat and Holland nodded me in beside him. The Lieutenant squeezed in last and got the door shut. We pulled away from the curb.

"You didn't really think I'd be heeled, did you," I said, "in a strange town?"

"Just routine," Holland grunted.

"Not such a strange town," Gimpy said. "Like all other towns—maybe a little cleaner."

We turned a couple of corners and rolled past City Hall. Pretty soon we were angling away from downtown, past the old Plaza and out beyond the post office. Holland settled back in the seat and lit a cigarette.

"I understand Porter fired you," he said.

"You've got good lines," I said.

"We don't do so bad," Gimpy said, "for a hick town. Of course, we don't have the heavy experience you boys had in Chicago."

"This is a *private* policeman," Holland said.

Gimpy's eyebrows flew up. "He *is?* Well, what do you know about that? No kidding. You one of these private eyes, goes around helping poor people?"

"No," I said. "Just rich people."

"What did Porter hire you for in the first place?" Holland asked.

"I can't tell you," I said.

"You mean you don't even know?" Gimpy was all surprise again.

"I mean I can't tell you."

"He means," Holland explained, "that if he tells us, he breaks the sacred code of his—profession?"

"Oh," Gimpy said solemnly. "They got a code too, huh?"

These two made quite a team. They took turns playing comic and straight man, so you were never quite sure which one to watch out for. I looked out the window, but nothing in the unfamiliar landscape gave me a clue as to where we were going.

Gimpy's elbow dug into my ribs. He leaned close. "Come on!" he urged, very confidential, "what was wrong in Porter's household? It'll never get past the Lieutenant and me."

"I do not know," I said, spacing the words enough to be firm, but without intending disrespect. "I do not know who killed Bernie Wolf. I will be glad to repeat anything I've told you before."

"All right," Holland said. "It's a start."

"From the beginning?"

"Why not?"

So I told them, as before, and it took about thirty seconds. We were up in some hills now, drifting past dark houses. Holland spoke to the driver and we stopped.

CHAPTER TWELVE

It was an old development, high up over the city. The houses looked well-kept and expensive. They were very large houses, bordered and screened by adult trees and foliage. The air was cooler than down below, even a little raw, but that could have been my emotional condition.

"That's quite a story," Gimpy said cheerfully.

"It's the best I can do," I said.

Lieutenant Holland lit a cigarette, broke the match, held it till it stopped smoking and tossed it out the window.

"Bernie Wolf had a cleaning woman—came in twice a week," he said; "colored girl name of Ruth. Seemed to have it in her head that Bernie had a girl-friend."

"Only one?" I said. "He was a good-looking bachelor and he made good money. He had a lot of glamorous contacts."

"One particular girl-friend," Holland said, "very hush-hush."

"What was her name?"

Gimpy chuckled. "Man, I tell you, these P.I.s are thinking all the time. We were going to ask you that very question," he said.

"I didn't know Bernie that well," I said.

"Tonight, when you left Porter's," Holland said, "Mrs. Porter left too. It looked as if Porter was cleaning house altogether."

"I wasn't watching as close as you," I said.

"I spent a lot of time the last few days thinking about Bernie Wolf," Holland said. "I see a guy in a good spot. Besides the high pay—which he earned it—he gets certain other advantages. Like he gets Julie's Cadillac every year when Julie gets a new one. Probably half-price he gets it. Then a big man like Julie, he gets a lot of loot at Christmas—cases of whiskey, champagne and a lot of stuff, all of which he can't use completely. So Bernie gets some of that—like hand-me-downs, see?"

"I don't doubt it," I said.

"So there are maybe other types of hand-me-downs and a fella like Bernie would be a sucker not to take advantage of them. Certain types of women might come under the heading of hand-me-downs. But that would have to be hush-hush, because a sensitive fella like Bernie couldn't let it out that he was sleeping with his boss's former wives or girl-friends."

"I don't know," I said. "Bernie was good enough to do his own hunting. But so if you're right?"

"So tonight, when Julie Porter threw you out, how come he threw Carol out too?"

Gimpy giggled. "Maybe she was a private eye too," he said. "Female type."

His timing was a little off on that one and Holland looked unhappy. It had come off as comic relief rather than needling.

"Exactly what happened," I said, "was this. I was in bed. Julie was out somewhere. Carol knocked at my door and came in. She said she had to talk to me. I asked her to get dressed and I'd meet her downstairs. She was upset. We argued about it. I finally won the argument. I was showing her out, when Julie came upstairs. He blew his stack. Very normal reaction. A couple of days, he'll probably get over it."

"Because naturally," Gimpy said, "there was nothing to it."

"That's right," I said.

"Sure," Holland said. "Nothing happened. The blonde just came to your bedroom in her nightie to pass the time of day and it was all a big misunderstanding."

I kept quiet. It was the way I wanted them to think. It was a natural tack that would carry them a long way before they could come about and get going in another direction.

Gimpy gave me the elbow again. "Now come on," he said. "Who was Bernie Wolf's girl-friend?"

"I don't know," I said.

"Maybe that governess of Porter's," he said. "Miss Rummel?"

I said I thought not.

"You never can tell about those prissy types," he said.

"True," I said, "but she keeps pretty busy."

"What did Carol want to talk about?" Holland said.

"She never got around to it," I said. "I didn't give her a chance."

"A shame," Gimpy said.

"Didn't Julie hire you to keep an eye on Carol?" Holland said.

"I can't say," I said.

I couldn't let myself believe in the good way things were going. We were bound to hit an outside curve any minute. Until then, we could all hang in and hope for the best.

"I mean," Holland pursued it, "after Julie's experience with the former Mrs. Porter, he might want a watchdog on the premises. Those ex-wives are pretty expensive, unless you can get something on them."

That was when we hit the curve. I could feel myself lurching between them. Because suddenly I knew where we were. Holland's latest innuendo, combined with stray conversations of the recent past, placed us in the neighborhood of the former Mrs. Porter—Gen Richards and her brother, Paulie "Velvet Gloves" Richards.

It was a real blind curve. Even if Holland and Gimpy reasoned that Gen Richards had been Bernie's hand-me-down girl and had killed him, I couldn't figure out what they hoped to gain by bringing *me* to her.

It is to learn we live.

* * * *

Lieutenant Holland opened the car door.

"Let's go visiting," he said.

As we climbed out, Gimpy gabbled happily at me. "We would run you back to your hotel," he said, "only we got a call to make up here and no use makin' an extra trip on the taxpayers' time."

"Sure," I said.

"Besides," he said, "you might be able to give us a few pointers, you know, Chicago style? We're just hick-town cops."

He was beginning to get to me and I had trouble swallowing the obvious retort.

We walked up the silent street, leaving the car behind. The large home on the curve above us was dark. As we rounded the shoulder on which it perched, I saw lights in the next house, a little lower, more rambling. On a mailbox at the street was the name "Richards" and a number.

We climbed a curving driveway, bordered by overgrown, untended shrubbery. Paint had peeled off the wood siding and the entry portals and there were grass-filled cracks in the cement stones approaching the door. Hard times encrusted the house like scales.

The Lieutenant pushed a button and a gonglike bell sounded inside. The door finally opened a few inches and Gen Richards looked out at us, her subtly ravaged face yellowed by the dusty porch light. Gimpy flipped a card as a matter of habit.

"Police—" he said.

Gen kept looking at me. "Come in," she said.

Single file, with me in the middle, we followed her inside. She was wearing faded pink velvet Capri pants and a white blouse and her hair was tied loosely in back with a pink ribbon. Her shoulders were a little stooped.

We walked into a living room with a bare floor and a minimum of furniture. Newspapers were scattered about. There was a smell of stale food. No windows were open that I could see. Paulie was sprawled in an armchair with his feet on an ottoman and a drink in his hand, watching the tag end of a very late, very old movie on the TV.

"Sit down," Gen said. "He won't talk till the show's finished."

"No hurry," Holland said. "All right if we smoke?"

"Sure," she said.

She sat down on a tattered love seat, folded her legs under her tightly and waited. The softer, shaded light of the living room flattered her. She caught me looking at her and returned the look for a moment, then glanced away.

"How's Linda?" she asked.

"Fine," I said.

Music swelled thinly, marking the end of the movie and I heard a click as Paulie Richards turned off the TV.

"Some gentlemen to see you," Gen said.

Paulie took a drink, looked around lazily and blinked at us. "Oh—hi, Lieutenant," he said. "What I do?"

"Hello, Paulie," Gimpy said. "This how you train?"

"For bums," Paulie said. "All bums."

"Like that last one you mangled?"

"I threw that fight," he said. "The bum had a sick mother."

"Excuse me," Gimpy said.

Paulie got up, stretching. He wore black, high-waisted slacks and a white shirt with a Lord Byron collar. It set him off. There was nothing pug-like about him. A lock of thick, curly black hair fell across his forehead. He liked it that way. I had heard that some of his Mexican fans, especially the ladies, referred to him as "Torero," and how he had actually considered a career in bullfighting, had spent time in Mexico City. He had the physical plant for it, but the language and the tradition had beaten him. According to the way I had heard it.

"Fix you guys something?" he said.

We shook our heads.

"So what do you want, huh?" he said. "You want Gen to blow?"

"No, no," Holland said. "We'd like to talk to her too."

"So talk." Paulie stretched again, did a couple of knee bends and flexed his hands. Big hands. Otherwise he was deceptively slight for a light-heavy-weight.

"On the way up here," Holland said, "we were talking it over about Bernie Wolf."

"You remember Bernie," Gimpy said.

"Uh-huh," Paulie said. "Good guy."

Holland turned to Gen. "Of course, you knew Bernie," he said.

Gen carefully lifted her left hand, folded her fingers down over her palm and looked at her nails. "We went over this once before," she said.

"Well you know how it is. We have to keep hashing it over until we find the right answer."

"Lucky for us," Gimpy put in, "we picked up some expert help. This gentleman here is from Chicago. He's one of these private eyes, you heard of them. They know more different ways to go about these things than us ordinary policemen."

Both Gen and her brother were looking at me. Gimpy had got back his sense of timing. "Besides which," he said, "he's been living with Julie Porter for a couple of weeks, so he picked up quite a lot of inside dope."

Holland took over, right on schedule. "What we were doing," he said, "we were talking it over about Bernie with special attention to his sex life."

Gen Richards, without taking her eyes off me, lowered her elbow to the arm of the settee, opened her fist and leaned her cheek on her hand.

"And the private investigator," Gimpy was saying, "came up with a very interesting theory." Paulie Richards sat down on the ottoman and massaged his hands between his spread knees. Under the drooping lock of hair, his eyes brooded at me. Until now, there hadn't been any way to know if he was listening.

I could guess now where they were taking me. It was quite a trick and it looked as if they could bring it off. I had three choices that added up to no choice at all. I could point out that they were on the wrong track and explain why; I could indignantly deny the words they were about to put in my mouth; or I could make a run for it. The last was futile because I couldn't run all the way to Chicago. The second was silly, wouldn't be believed. The first was merely out of the question.

"His theory," Gimpy was saying, "is that one of Julie's wives might have done Bernie in, because we all know that Bernie and Julie were like this—" with the crossed fingers—"I mean, like with hand-me-downs—well, you know what I mean."

He might have meant a number of things. But it didn't matter. He wasn't out to mean anything, only to plant a small bomb.

One of the oldest clichés of fiction refers to how "the color drained slowly from her face." Gen Richards' face didn't have much color to start with, so it didn't react in that way. It closed, the way shutters close, stiff, board-like. The hand supporting her head didn't move, but something happened to it because the knuckles went white as if she were pressing very hard. Later, when she took her hand away, I could see the marks it had left on her cheek.

The change in brother Paulie was more primitive, also more obvious. From idly massaging his fighter's hands, he turned to making experimental fists, shadowboxing a phantom between his knees. He even vocalized some, in a suppressed monotone, something between a growl and a mumble.

"Lieutenant," he said, "we talked about this once before, remember, about where we were that day when Bernie got it—Gen and me both."

"I know, Paulie," Holland said, "but we have to follow up every lead."

"All right," Paulie said, "suppose you go ahead and follow it up and get the hell out of here, huh?"

He wasn't looking at me anymore, but I was still there, unmistakably.

"Take it easy, Paulie," Gimpy said soothingly. "Nobody said anything much."

"I never had any beef against Bernie and you know that, Lieutenant."

"Sure, Paulie," Holland said. "We weren't saying you had."

"Neither did Gen."

"Maybe not," Holland said, "but somebody had a beef against him. You could see that real plain."

It had gone about as far as it could go without something snapping. They had given Paulie one end of a long strip of rubber and stretched it tight and glued the other end to me. Paulie was the only one who could let go.

With a gambler's instinct, he held on. Like a boy reciting an old lesson, he spoke to the detectives, studiously avoiding me. "That day," he said, "I was in three, four different places. Like I told you. I worked out at the Main Street gym. Ten o'clock till eleven-thirty. I went over to the Hollywood Center and had lunch with three guys. After lunch we went—"

Holland's hand was up, waving gently. "Yeah, Paulie. We checked it all out."

"So what do you want from me?"

Gimpy's marvelous timing came into play again. "Don't be nervous, Paulie," he said, and looked at Gen.

Everybody except me looked at Gen. But I couldn't close my ears. In a low voice, monotonous, faintly guttural, she said, "I never fooled around with Bernie. I wasn't what you would call the most faithful wife in the world, but never with Bernie. Bernie and I hardly spoke to each other. But we got along."

"Besides which," Paulie said, speaking faster now with a hard edge, "we went over where Gen was that day too, Lieutenant."

"Yeah," Holland said slowly, "we did. Of course, she said she spent most of the day at home, alone. There wasn't really any way to check it out—"

"All right," the fighter said. "But you got to prove it if it wasn't so and if you had any proof you wouldn't be sitting around here like this."

Holland and Gimpy got on their feet. Gimpy came in with the soothing syrup again. "Hold your horses, Paulie. Maybe we're barking up the wrong tree. We just have to check out every possibility, and when this private eye here came up with his theory—after all he was right in Julie's home and all—"

"Getting late," Holland said, "sorry we kept you up."

I got up carefully and started with them to the door. Paulie's eyes, half-closed, followed us step by step. I didn't look at Gen.

"Hey!" Gimpy said suddenly. "Since we're up here, seems like a shame to go without showing this fellow from out of town around your place."

Paulie blinked at him once, then got the idea. I remember his getting it at that moment—because he was a very bright kid—and that I didn't get it until a few seconds later.

"Sure," Paulie said.

Gimpy nudged me. "Kid's got his own private gym in the basement," he said. "You ought to see that. He's fixed it up real nice. Got a regulation-size ring and everything."

"Well," I said, "it's late, as the Lieutenant said—"

"I guess we got that much time," Holland said, "if Paulie doesn't mind."

"Sure," Paulie repeated. "Come on."

He moved ahead of us, light on his feet now, with the skilled, economical grace of the born athlete, young and vital. I was getting the idea then myself and, as earlier, I could see no way out.

CHAPTER THIRTEEN

The layout must have cost him a young fortune, but I recalled that he had made a generous potful in his time. Then, too, Gen would have been married to Julie Porter at the time and it probably had looked as if there would always be plenty for everybody. High-powered frosted lights shone on an array of expensive equipment: barbells, Indian clubs, chest weights, a heavy bag and the light punching sack; lockers lined one wall, and the whole set was dominated by the big boxing ring in the center, complete to corner stools, water buckets and two or three rows of chairs at ringside.

Paulie escorted us on a tour, moving a little ahead, light and springy on the balls of his feet, now and then pointing something out. I admired everything in a reserved way. We had made three-fourths of the circuit around the walls when I saw Gen leaning in a doorway, her arms folded, watching us with the typical expression of the female observing the boys at play. I tried to catch her eye and she managed to make it impossible.

Gimpy got me with the elbow again. "Some layout?"

"Great," I said.

Paulie turned around and his shut was unbuttoned. He headed for the row of lockers, pulling the shirt off as he went. "Go a couple rounds, huh?" he said.

I pretended not to hear. Once more the elbow, and I re-minded myself to get Gimpy alone some night and do some sandpapering on his joint.

"Go ahead," Gimpy urged. "Go a couple of rounds with the kid. You're in good shape."

"Me?" I said.

"I don't know," Holland said. "The private eye is maybe more of a talker."

Gimpy shrugged. "Well, if you'd rather have some more conversation—" So it was clear enough. I could come across with what they wanted to know or I could mix it up with Velvet Gloves, possibly for the rest of the night. Any broken hands that might result from the session would not belong to the police. It was a roundabout way of getting to me, but it could be very effective. Watching the young fighter, stripped to his trim waist, I felt the hard truth of his ironic nickname. I had boxed in my time and had fought, occasionally for my life, and, when aroused, I still had some heart. But my legs and my wind were an old man's, and the younger guy could jab me to jelly while I was running away.

"This seems a little ridiculous," I said.

"Yeah," Holland said, "I guess so. What was that you were going to say—about Bernie Wolf's girl-friend?"

Gimpy's fingers fumbled at my jacket, unbuttoned it.

"You're crazy," Gen Richards said quietly. "You and all men are blind crazy."

Gimpy had my coat, carrying it toward one of the lockers. "I'll hang it up over here so it won't get wrinkled," he said.

Holland gave me a light push toward the ring. "Go ahead," he said. "The kid won't hurt you. Give him a little workout. I've heard you're tough."

Paulie Richards was waiting beside the ring. I took off my necktie and got out of my shirt. He measured me briefly and grinned. "Here," he said. "No sense banging ourselves up."

He tossed me a pair of gloves. Well—pads; the tight, thin gloves they wear for working out on the bags. They protect the knuckles, the flesh of the hands. He was giving me that much break. He was very young and lacking in wisdom. But as chairman of the entertainment committee, it was his right. Holland, watching, looked a little nervous, but he had let it come this far.

With a catlike spring, Paulie vaulted to the apron, then climbed through the ropes and danced, shadowboxing around the magic square. Holland laced and tied my gloves. I let him. There wasn't any dignified alternative. I couldn't run and hope to get away. I couldn't take on all three of them. I couldn't talk. I could hope to stay away from Paulie Richards and ride it out until they all got tired of it. I could hope, but I couldn't figure on it.

As I climbed into the ring, Velvet Gloves stopped his dancing and retired to lean on the ropes. He wasn't grinning any more. His eyes had that half-shut, brooding look. Beyond him, in the doorway, slouching with folded arms, Sister Gen looked on. Down at one side, Gimpy was crouched over the bell, his face alight. Holland looked on solemnly from the other side of the ring.

"Two-minute rounds okay?" Gimpy said.

Paulie nodded.

"Okay with you, Mr. Pinkerton?" Gimpy said..

I shrugged. Stripped to the waist, I felt naked white under the strong lights. Paulie, the Californian, was brown as the gloves he wore. His hands flexed nervously in the skimpy pads.

"Skip the formalities," he said. "Go ahead."

He wouldn't look at me. He was on no lark. He had a grudge. I had insulted his sister and called his own alibi to account, so they had told him. This was his chance to lay a few on me with official sanction, and the best I could hope for was that I could prevent his laying on too many. The tendons of my hams were tight as stretched wire.

"Okay—? Go!" Gimpy said.

The bell clanged brassily in the big room. Paulie floated across the ring to meet me, his dukes up, relaxed. He didn't bother with showing off; no ducking or weaving. He came in, watching my face, his left out for the jab. I could box with him or I could stand flat on my feet and try to hold him off and get knocked out of my skin.

Because this boy was fast. The left went for my head and was nudging my chest when I ducked. His right hooked into the side of my face twice and I hadn't laid a glove on him. He didn't intend I should. When I made a pass he stiffened his arms and backed off. I dealt him a glancing blow on the ribs and found I had a little reach on him. I moved in to see about mixing it up close and he hit my head five times, left and right. I backed off, slipping in my street shoes on the slick canvas. That let him score three or four points and my head began to ring.

The top rope seared my back and I grabbed it with one hand to keep from slipping to the floor. He slugged me hard in the neck and again on the ear, then danced off backward, beckoning me with both gloves. I glanced down and Gimpy was hugging the bell, gazing up with a beautiful smile.

I went in to meet the boy, ducked a left and tied him up. He slapped me a couple of times low on the back and his chin dug into my shoulder.

"You got any more bright theories about my sister?" he muttered.

I didn't say anything. I didn't have the breath for it. He pushed me off and danced in, jabbing and hooking, and I managed to bat most of them down and pretty soon the bell rang. He clouted my ear as I turned away toward one of the corners.

The second round wasn't so bad, except that he had started working on my nose and he was moving around me all the time, keeping me off balance and winded. He had found the range and his grudge wasn't working itself off. It was building up. Even with the sweat clouding my vision, I could predict some of his punches by the look in his eyes. I got him in a clinch and tried to gasp a brief message, saying, "The cops have steered you wrong. It wasn't my idea—"

But he didn't want to hear that. The back of his head came up under my chin and rocked me back into the ropes. He followed through and let me have it in a fast flurry and I got in one good one under his heart that twisted him. But he came back, furious, and jabbed at my nose till the blood trickled down to my lip. Along in there it started turning into a fight and Gimpy plied his gong till we quit.

When I sank down on the stool, Holland leaned through the ropes and handed up a wet sponge. I cleaned my nose and lip and Holland said, "The kid's kind of sore. Maybe we ought to call it off."

"Any time," I said, panting.

"You want to talk things over?"

"Not your way," I said. "I can't and you must know it."

"No such thing," he said.

He jerked his head and the gong clanged loudly. Paulie came three-fourths of the way across the ring and I got up slowly and moved crabwise out of his reach, circling him. He came in and jabbed some and I protected my nose at the expense of my ears and chin.

After half a minute of this, with the sour, metallic windlessness in my throat and the backs of my legs laced with red-hot cord, I knew that in a fair fight he could kill me—and might, if they didn't stop it in time. The fair fight was over with. The rules would be suspended. He was a young pro and I was an old amateur. It was going to be a shame because I had nothing against him—except that he kept slapping my nose and it was bleeding again.

He had that left in my face, chopping and poking and his right hammering my ribs. I caught his left in both hands, raising it. So he swayed in to me and I kneed him sharply. He grunted and looked surprised. I got one foot up in his groin and gave it what I had, using the ropes for leverage. He stumbled backward across the ring and bounced off the opposite ropes. The gong started clanging furiously. Paulie returned, fighting, but he had been well conditioned to the rules and he came out boxing. I side-stepped as he reached me and kicked him back of the left knee. He floundered down on both knees and reached for me. I chopped hard at the back of his neck, then pulled him up, pushing him toward a corner. The gong was going crazy. Somebody shouted. Chasing Paulie, I saw Holland's hands on the mat, his shoulders poking under the rope as he climbed toward us. I stepped on one of his hands and he yipped and withdrew. Gen Richards was screaming.

In the corner, Paulie rallied enough to clip the side of my head. I hooked at his chin and he ducked back, banging his head on the corner post. I backed off a step to test whether he'd had enough. He flew at me, slugging. His face was bloody and I aimed for the blood with my right. He was hitting me once in a while but the sting was gone. He tried to tie me up in a clinch and I put my knee to his solar plexus. He arched out from me. I broke his clinch grip and belted his jaw. He went back on the ropes, clinging. I was following through when I noticed the gong was no longer clanging. At the same moment I felt the mat vibrating. When I swung around, Gimpy was there with an Indian club over his head. I saw Holland beyond him, closing in. My feet slipped when I ducked and the club came down, missing the hard part of my skull and connecting high on my nose between my eyes. All the lights changed color and went out.

* * * *

They came on again after a couple of minutes. My head buzzed with nausea. My nose throbbed dully and was no good for breathing. I rolled my eyes down and saw the ragged ends of a couple of cotton plugs. My face was damp and cold. They had covered me with my suit jacket. The smooth crust of the mat was warm under my shoulders. Holland squatted beside me. Beyond him, Gimpy approached with my shirt and tie.

I looked the other way. Gen Richards was holding her brothers head over a sink.

I rolled over, got my hand under me and prepared to be sick. When it didn't happen, I pushed on up to my feet. Gimpy would have held my shirt and coat for me, but I grabbed them and got into them alone. With my plugged nose, my voice sounded far off and unfamiliar.

"Is the kid all right?" I said.

"Uh-huh," Holland said. "You all right?"

"Oh sure," I said.

"Come on," Gimpy said. "Let's blow."

No more quips from Gimpy? I thought.

There was a steady, hot throbbing in the front of my head, but the buzzing had quieted. When I crossed the ring to get down, my knees were shaking. I held tight to the ropes, let myself down and made my way to one of the corners. I looked across to where Paulie was dousing his face with both hands, shouldering Gen aside. She leaned against the wall with her arms folded, looking at nothing much. Holland and Gimpy joined me.

"Come on—" Gimpy said again.

"No explanation for the lady?" I said.

"What explanation?" Holland said.

I caught Gen Richards' eye and shrugged. Speaking muffledly under the nose plugs, I said, "It was all a dreadful mistake."

She looked away. Holland took hold of my arm and I pulled it free gently. He didn't make anything of it.

"So long, Paulie," I said.

He kept his face in the sink. Holland and Gimpy led the way out of the house and down the drive. The cool air was bracing. But in the car, as we rode down from the hills into the city, the second reaction set in, the hard pain, blood in my throat and the persistent nausea. I was vaguely aware that Holland and Gimpy said things from time to time, but I took no part in the conversation. The way things were now, if they had asked me the time of day…

* * * *

When I asked the hotel physician the time of day he told me politely that it was four-fifteen in the morning, that he had gotten to bed two hours before and that he didn't mind at all getting out of bed to take care of some guy who had wandered around the low part of town and got himself beaten up.

He was pretty nice, though, before he went away. He said he thought my nose wasn't broken, that I had no broken ribs and no concussion and he just happened to have some painkillers on him that I should take a couple of and go to sleep and he would look in later in the day.

"Thanks," I said. "What time is it?"

"I told you," he said.

"Oh yeah. Sorry to get you out at this hour," I said.

"Think nothing of it. I'm a doctor. My business is to take care of the sick, any time, any place."

"Well, I'm not exactly sick."

"I couldn't say," he said.

"Isn't that your business?"

"Not in the way I presumed you meant."

"Oh. Well—thanks again. How much do I owe you?"

"I'll leave a bill at the desk," he said.

"Very good," I said.

I hated to see him go. It was lonely and desolate in the hotel room. I was scared. I couldn't put my finger on it, but I was afraid someone would come in and finish me off while I slept.

After he had gone, I tossed the pills in my hand and thought it over for a while and finally I decided the only way to get rid of the fear was to knock myself out. If anything was going to happen, I'd be better off not to know about it.

But nothing happened. I slept all right and I guess it helped, but I had some lousy dreams. Most of them were about Bernie Wolf. Then there were some other people mixed up in it, some of whom I had known years before and who had no connection with Bernie or Julie Porter or Carol or any of these others.

I woke up hard and slowly and while I was getting that done, I spent a lot of time thinking about Bernie—about the way I had found him dead in the big chair, the hole in the side of his head, the gun loose in his fingers; the way Carol had looked, white as a bleached skull and the blue stain on her fingers and the funny way she looked at it.

She had had a lot of guts, that one, scared as she was. Either she knew she was innocent and hoped for the best, or, if she had killed him, she had figured me on her side.

And I wondered what she had held out on me.

But Bernie had been holding something out too.

And maybe some of the others.

For how many different reasons? I wondered. And how good?

I ordered up some breakfast. When it came, I gagged over it, got the coffee down and went back to bed. I slept until about eleven o'clock and the telephone woke me. It was the desk calling.

"We have your plane reservation," the clerk said.

"What plane reservation?"

"American Airlines to Chicago," he said. 'We've just received a call confirming it."

"Oh," I said. "Yeah. Thanks very much."

I got up slowly, painfully, took a long shower, put on some clothes and went downstairs. I had to walk carefully to keep my nose from running blood.

I walked up the dingy morning street to a cigar store and into a telephone booth. I called American Airlines at the airport. They confirmed my reservation again.

"When did I make it?" I asked.

"It's for tonight, Flight 316—"

"No, I mean when did I order it?"

"I beg your pardon?"

"I mean where did I call from?"

"You don't remember making the call, sir?"

"No. I was out some last night."

"The call came from your hotel, sir."

"What time?"

"About three-thirty this morning."

I remembered Holland and Gimpy letting me out of the car and driving away, after making sure I could get to my room without the telltale nose plugs. They could have driven around the block, come into the hotel and made the call to the airport.

"Was there some question, sir?" the girl was saying.

"Oh—no. Cancel it."

"Cancel the reservation, sir?"

"Yeah, please. I guess I was drunk."

"Very good, sir," she said crisply, and hung up.

I sat in the booth for a while, sweating lightly and then I chopped a dime in the slot and dialed Julie Porter's home. The thing rang a dozen times. Then there was a loud click and Sophie's voice exploded in my ear.

"Yeah? Hello! Who is it?"

"Hello, Sophie?"

"Yeah, Sophie. Who is it?"

"Sophie, I'd like to speak to Miss Rummel."

"What?"

"Miss Rummel—Alice."

"No, she ain't home now. Goodbye."

"Wait a minute, please—"

"Hey, who is it?" A lethal pause. "You—Mr. Mac—"

"A—yeah, Sophie—"

"You! Hang up on me! You got a big nerve calling up in the broad daylight…"

She lapsed into German and went on for quite a while. When she finally stopped to breathe, I said, "I just wanted to speak to Miss Rummel, Sophie—"

"Das ist alles! Goodbye!" she said.

The receiver banged down irrevocably.

I walked up the street to a coffee shop and took on a little fuel. Unlike the earlier breakfast, it went down and stayed. Most of the discomfort from the brawl with Paulie had leveled off to a general stiffness, but I still had that mushy, uncertain feeling in my nose and sinuses.

Three times during the meal I went to a phone booth and called the Wilshire Boulevard hotel where I had heard Carol direct her cab the night before. She wasn't registered under the name "Porter" and although they had a guest named "Carol Collins," either she was out or was not accepting any calls.

The eating or the exertion or something had started the flow in my nose and I had to stuff it again after leaving the cafe. Then I got into a taxi and rode out Wilshire to the sedate old hotel and started hanging around.

CHAPTER FOURTEEN

I hung around from two o'clock until five—strolling on the street, sitting in the lobby or prowling through the three cocktail lounges at various levels of the establishment. It was a quiet, discreetly managed hotel on a quiet day and by the time I was ready to give up, it had nearly lulled me to sleep.

But I was awake enough to spot her, dark glasses notwithstanding, when she came through the lobby a little after five and walked with her swinging, arrogant young stride into the most intimate of the three taverns and sat down in a dim, isolated corner. She was wearing a smart, ultra-fashionable afternoon dress, her grooming was impeccable, and you couldn't possibly have guessed from her appearance what she had experienced the previous evening.

When I spoke to her from across the little table, her eyes widened for a moment behind the glass veils, but it was the only chink in the bright armor of her poise.

"May I?" I said, and she nodded.

A waiter came and when he had gone, she got out a cigarette and I lit it for her. The drinks came and the fellow wandered away and she took a long drag on the cigarette. Then she said, "Before you say anything, let's get it straight that I'm not on the town."

"All right," I said.

"And one more thing," she said, "I'm not in line for any reconciliation pitch or any such crap as that."

I took a sip of my drink. "That's a very interesting remark," I said.

She shrugged lightly. "That's why you're here, isn't it?" she said. "That's why you were hired in the first place, wasn't it? To keep an eye on the restless young wife?"

I didn't say anything and she took the glasses off and looked at me. "Well?" she said. "Wasn't it? All that melodramatic stuff about Linda—" She let it trail off.

"Go ahead," I said, "it's getting more interesting all the time. That same identical suggestion was made a few hours ago, by a couple of policemen."

If that gave her a start, she hid it perfectly.

"These policemen," I said, "had developed a theory that Bernie Wolf's murder had something to do with a woman."

"Nothing unusual in that, I guess," she said. "There's an old French phrase I seem to remember."

"I think they have a little more to go on than an old phrase. They have some testimony from Bernie's cleaning woman. Apparently, they have some evidence that an unknown woman—presumably with an intimate attachment to Bernie—was in his apartment at the time of his death, or almost at that time. They suspect that she was spirited away in such a manner as to conceal the fact that she had been there. They also suspect that I may have had a hand in this. They would like to know who the woman was."

She was giving me full attention now, direct, deadpan. "You mean they don't know yet?" she said.

"Not yet."

She finished her cocktail and I signaled for the waiter. He brought us another round, unobtrusively and with dispatch. Her eyes studied my face over the rim of the glass.

"How hard did they try to find out?" she asked.

"Not too hard. Something went wrong."

We did some more drinking. She was getting ahead of me and I was willing that she should. There's an old Latin phrase about truth and wine.

"Well," she said finally, elaborately casual, "what are you doing here? I'm sure you didn't come to me in order to save your own skin. You're not the type."

"What type do you think I am?"

She studied me; her mouth twitched, then stiffened. She was in no mood to be amused if she could help it. "I don't know," she said. "The strong, silent, fatherly type. How's that?"

"All right," I said, "put me down as fatherly. I can't seem to help giving advice."

She sighed and twirled her empty glass, handling the fragile stem with clean, red-tipped fingers. I ordered her another drink.

"Go ahead," she said. "As long as it's free."

"Assuming you didn't shoot Bernie, unless you establish yourself in the clear, you are heading into unpleasantness."

"In the near future?"

"My guess would be very near—like tonight, or tomorrow or the next day. But eventually these policemen will be around to see you. If you tell them the true facts and stick to it, I doubt that anything much will come of it."

"And if I don't tell them the facts?"

"They'll find out anyway. They're very close. They may have finger-prints in the mill right now, prints we overlooked; they may have something else. If they have to find out by themselves that you were there and they don't find any other more likely suspect, they'll go to work to build a case."

"Then what?"

"You'd probably be acquitted, if you're innocent. But it would be nasty and time-consuming to go through it—and unnecessary."

She lit another cigarette. As far as I could tell, she was still unshaken.

"Do you think I killed Bernie?" she asked.

"No," I said. "But all I have to go on is your word, your alibi and the fact that as far as I can tell, you didn't have any motive. That's enough for me, but I'm not a policeman or a prosecutor."

She gazed into the pristine depths of her martini. I was reminded of the remark of a friend who once said, "I looked into that martini and all the events of my life passed in review." I'd have defied an authentic mind reader to describe what was passing in Carol's martini. When she looked up her eyes were as bland and opaque as on that night I had first seen her, briefly waking, in the plane that was taking us to Los Angeles.

"What makes you so sure I didn't have a motive?" she said.

"I'm not sure. I mean only that if you had, I don't know what it was."

"Any guesses?"

"Unh-uh. I'm not much of a guesser."

"I guess you're not," she said.

A little time went by. She was two-thirds of the way through her third martini and her lips had relaxed a little. When she looked at me again, the corners of her mouth twitched some more and she didn't fight so hard for solemnity.

"So your advice is for me to tell the police about being there—in Bernie's apartment."

"I would do that if I were in your shoes."

She looked me over with a sidelong glance. "You'd look pretty silly in my shoes."

"No doubt," I said.

"On the other hand, I don't look especially silly in my own shoes, because they fit."

I depended on silence to discourage the repartee.

"What I'm getting at," she said, "is that I don't think it would be very smart to tell the police anything right now."

"Well, it's up to you," I said.

"It is? I should think part of it would be up to you. Why didn't you tell them? Last night, or whenever it was. If they were hurting you—"

"They weren't hurting me."

"What would they do to you if they found out you had 'spirited' me away, as you call it, and tried to conceal the whole thing? That's kind of a crime, isn't it?"

"In a way."

"Then what? Aren't you a law-abiding citizen?"

"More or less. At that time I was in the employ of your husband. By a narrow interpretation, I had no responsibility to you. But that's pretty narrow interpreting."

"Well, last night changed everything. So last night you were out from under."

"Not altogether."

"You're a strange kind of guy."

"I'm just a guy."

"No, I mean you have a kind of sense of something—like duty, something—"

"There's nothing so hard to understand about it."

"No, I mean I think I understand all right. All too well. I mean you're a disturbing influence."

I finished my drink, got out some money and covered the tab. "Okay," I said. "I guess that's it. I didn't come to disturb you. Sorry."

I started up and she slid her hand to my arm. "Come on," she said, "don't sulk for goodness' sake. So you tried to help me and I kicked your teeth in, or out. Sit down and buy me another drink."

So now it would come, I thought. And maybe it wouldn't take too long.

"That's a good boy," she said. "I'm going to tell you something, because you're a nice guy and kind of rare."

"Not too rare. Julie's a nice guy when you learn how. Bernie was a nice guy."

"Bernie was a hell of a nice guy. The greatest."

The waiter brought us another round and she twirled the glass slowly with her long fingers.

"There wasn't anything between Bernie and me," she said, "except friendship. That is the honest to God truth, not that it matters. It might matter to you—I'm not sure about you." I shrugged.

"So anyway—as far as Julie was concerned, I hoped he would think there *was* something with Bernie. God knows I tried everything short of telling him." She paused for a sip of gin. "That may sound funny to you; after all you're a man. But you have to realize what Julie was. Like a machine. Big, powerful machine, complicated, sure, but specialized, to make pictures, nothing else.

"Maybe it's the same with any big businessman—successful type, I mean. But I don't think so. I don't think it's the same as making cars, or steel, or running a chain of banks. Because, making pictures, you never really know what you're doing until it's all done. You don't know what you've got, because it depends on so many people. So you worry most of the time—day and night. And that's Julie. I guess 'machine' is the wrong word. A machine doesn't worry.

"That's hard to live with, Mac. If you think I'm exaggerating, listen—on our honeymoon, without going into all the juicy details, on our very first night, Julie was talking and, being a little busy, I didn't listen too much at first. Then all of a sudden I realized he was telling me something about some damn picture! Right while—well... I remember, inside myself, in my head, thinking, 'It's *me* here, Julie. It's *me,* it's *me*—She broke off and it was like an amputation. It showed in her face.

"I mean," she said quietly, "I don't mean that's all there is to marriage. It's just an example. The thing is—to live with Julie, for a woman, you have to get under his skin some way. Otherwise it's like living in a one-woman harem; or a flower in a pot that once in a while somebody sprinkles a little water on you."

"So," I said, for something to say, "you were in love with Julie when you married him?"

Carol ran her finger slowly around the rim of her glass. "You want to know my private, personal theory about love?" she said. "Love is a luxury. It's what you have left over after the bills are paid. It's a windfall—like an unexpected dividend; or when they split the stock and suddenly you've got twice as much. And you know something else? The only people who get love, or even deserve to get it, are lovable people. I don't mean perfect people, or special or brilliant or rich and famous or magnetic or proud or beautiful. I just mean lovable."

"That makes it sort of mysterious," I said.

"Sure it's mysterious. And you try to make it something else—like the patter of tiny feet or bread and salt on the table or some certain way to be-have or not to behave—and you'll never know what it is; or you'll kill it."

She broke off again and took out another cigarette, handling it with stiff, jerky movements.

"My," she said, "I'm quite a philosopher all of a sudden. I could write a play."

"Was Bernie one of the lovable ones?" I asked.

She nodded. "One of the most. Not that it paid off much for him. Just being lovable doesn't mean you automatically get loved. Besides lovable, you have to be lucky." She looked at me quickly and looked away. "What do you want me to say?" she said.

"Nothing special."

"I guess I took off again, didn't I? I mean about Bernie—he was lovable but he didn't let it show much. He was—what?—too intelligent maybe. Always thinking. But once in a while, the way he would look at you…"

I no longer looked at her directly. There comes a time. "As I said," I told her, "whether you talk to the police or not is up to you. But it might help both of us if we could run through the details once more, just between us, so we both withhold the same facts."

"Sure," she said promptly, over-brightly. "When they finished with me at the beauty shop, I called Bernie at home."

"That was about three-fifteen?"

"Yes. There was no answer, so I called the studio. Julie was in a conference. Clarissa said Bernie hadn't come in. He had called earlier and said he would be home all afternoon. So I knew that sometimes Bernie just didn't answer his phone, if he didn't want to be disturbed, and I decided to just drop in."

"So you got there at about three-thirty."

She nodded. "He didn't come to the door when I knocked, so I used my key."

Inadvertently, our eyes met for a moment.

"By the way," she said, "what about that key?"

"I disposed of it," I said.

There was a look in her eye almost as if she knew I lied, but I knew it was something else. She had come to the hard part now.

"For a second," she said, "I thought he had fallen asleep in his chair. Then I saw the gun and the odd way he looked. I was so scared—it was like suddenly I didn't have any knees."

After a moment I prompted gently. "Then you went in." She nodded.

"And how long was it before you called me?"

"About five minutes."

"On Bernie's phone."

"Yes"

"Not the phone by his bed, the phone on the stand next to his chair."

She nodded hesitantly.

"Was the drawer of the stand open?"

"I beg your pardon?" she said.

"The stand by his chair," I said, "had a drawer. I looked into it and there were some papers, mail, one thing and another."

"Oh," she said.

"I asked whether the drawer was open—at the time you made the telephone call."

"I don't remember," she said.

But before, I thought, that day it happened, she had remembered all right. She had said it was open.

"You don't remember either opening or closing the drawer?"

"No," she said. "Why?"

"You were very fond of Bernie," I said. "You'd have done a lot for him."

"Bernie did a lot for me."

A small time passed. The cocktail lounge was filling up with quiet, well-dressed and somehow harried-looking people. Some of them were quite beautiful, in the same way Carol was beautiful, with the glorious hair, the tanned California skin.

"And there isn't anything else you'd like to tell me at this time?" I said. "About that day at Bernie's? Or afterward?"

She didn't answer and I didn't push it. When I looked at her, she was crying and it was like pink rain in her eyes. I wrote the name of my hotel and my room number on a cocktail napkin and put it in her hand.

"If you want me," I said, "in the next couple of days."

I started to get up and she said, still crying, "I tried to use Bernie to get to Julie. Instead of loving Bernie, which would have been easy and honest. And now Bernie's dead and I can't tell Julie anything about it. That's pretty funny, huh?" I touched her hand. It was warm and limp and the touch didn't say anything. There wasn't anything to say. Maybe what most of us do, we talk ourselves to death.

* * * *

At the hotel I went up to the room, took off my coat and shoes, fished some ice cubes out of the bowl and poured whiskey over them. I drank the slug and lay down on the bed with my hands under my head and thought about Bernie Wolf sitting dead in his chair with that stand beside him, and pretty soon there was a knock at the door.

I thought it might be the hotel doctor, just looking in; then I thought it might be the police. I lay very still, waiting for whichever it was to go away. After a while the knock came again, and a voice, a frail, ladylike voice, saying timidly, "Mac? It's me. Alice Hummel."

I got up then and went to the door in my stocking feet, switching on a lamp as I went.

CHAPTER FIFTEEN

Prim, a little frightened, she stood outside, waiting to be asked in. Her long fingers nervously massaged a small purse. She wore a light summer dress under a somewhat worn tweed topcoat. Her pale, blue eyes blinked, questioning. I looked up and down the corridor and saw she was alone. Her eyes moved away.

"I ran off," she said.

"Without Linda?"

"Linda's all right."

I stood back and she came in hesitantly, clutching the purse. I wondered whether she had ever before entered a hotel room with a man and no chaperon in sight. I was glad to see her, but felt a vague discomfort on her behalf.

"How did you know where I was?" I asked.

"Julie—Mr. Porter—had it written on a pad on his desk. Room number and all."

"Julie did?"

"There was a policeman came to the house about noon."

"Oh," I said.

She had seated herself on the edge of a chair near the window, knees together, her purse on her knees, her hands on the purse. There was an odd expectancy in her attitude. It made me nervous. When I moved about the room, I must have done it lamely.

"What happened?" she said. "You're hurt."

"Nothing," I said.

"You're hurt rather badly."

"Nothing that won't heal," I said. "I had a run-in with the local authorities."

Her face showed quiet horror. "You mean, the police—?"

"They were doing what they could. They thought Julie and I were holding out on them—about Bernie's murder. They couldn't very well get to Julie, so they settled for me."

"That's horrible. Can't you complain to someone? Bring charges?"

I started to laugh, but it hurt and I choked it off. I felt blood in my nose and excused myself hastily. When I came back from the bathroom, she was sitting as before except that she had set her purse on an end table and folded her hands on her knees.

"Did you quit Julie or what?" I asked.

"I guess I did."

"Does he know it? Did you tell him?"

"Yes. He was in his study, just—brooding, I guess. The door was open and I looked in and told him."

Her funny, soft, clipped accent had a hypnotic effect. When she saw I was waiting, listening, she went on with it. "I said, 'I'm sorry, I can't stay here. I'm leaving. I'll send for my things.' I said it fast, all at once, for fear I'd lose my nerve."

"And what did Julie say?"

"Nothing. He looked at me for a minute, then the telephone rang. He started talking with someone and paid no more attention to me. So I walked out."

"You didn't say goodbye to Linda?"

She looked at her hands. "No. I—couldn't."

"But you decided Linda would be all right."

"Yes. There was Sophie, and Mr. Porter—her own father, after all. I knew Julie—Mr. Porter—could call Mr. Walewski if he wanted to."

I nodded vaguely. We sat there, taking turns looking at each other, while the room darkened, slowly at first, then more rapidly. I finally managed to slap my thighs and get to my feet.

"Well," I said. Then I said, "How about a drink?"

She looked uncertain.

"I'm sorry the champagne isn't chilled," I said, "but I have some good whiskey."

She nodded jerkily, slant-eyed. "That will be fine," she said. "Just a little."

An extra glass had come with the ice I'd ordered earlier. There were a few wasted cubes still floating in the bowl and I scooped them into the glass along with some water and poured half a shot of whiskey in on top. In the midst of the pouring, my nose gave way again and before I could get my hands free and turn around, it was running on my lip.

Alice came up like a machine, moved past me into the bathroom and came back with clean tissue. While I held the bottle in one hand and the glass in the other, feeling ridiculous, she sponged with schooled expertness at my lip and nose.

"Thanks," I snuffled.

Her thin, anxious face reflected pain. I tried to hand her the glass, but she didn't take it. I put the bottle down.

"It's so swollen," she said. "Here, sit down." She gestured to an armchair and I sat in it. "Put your head back," she called from the bathroom.

She came in with a clean cloth and dipped it in the ice bowl, wrung it out and folded it carefully. I put my head back and she laid the pack carefully over the bridge of my nose, dabbed some more with the tissue and backed off.

"That may stop the flow," she said. "Try to sit still for a few minutes."

"Feels good," I said. "You're pretty good at this business."

"Is that my drink?" she said.

"Indeed."

She took it from me and backed off again, sipping at it, watching me with my head back.

"Do you think it's broken?" she asked.

"No. Just a couple of taps. Accidental."

"Accidental!"

"I tried to duck at the wrong time."

"Would you like a drink too?"

"I sure would."

"Just with water?"

"Just water."

She moved out of sight and I heard the bottle clinic lightly against something.

"How much whiskey?" she said. "I'm not much of a bar-keep."

I opened my hand, gesturing with thumb and forefinger. "That much."

She brought the glass over, set it against my human yardstick and blinked. "All that much?"

"If there is that much."

"Well—if you say so."

"I'm a sporadic drinker, not a lush," I said. "We'll have dinner in a few minutes. No harm done."

The stuff gurgled into the glass and she went to the bathroom for fresh tap water. I'd have preferred it out of the ice bucket, but she had dipped the cloth in there and I guessed her nurse's conditioning wouldn't let her use it for drinking.

She handed me the glass and did some fresh wringing of her compress and replaced it. The whiskey burned nicely going down. She hadn't put too much water in it and I decided she had sound instincts. We finished the highballs silently and I sat up experimentally, testing, and the blood flow had been stanched.

"I guess we'd better go out and celebrate our mutual freedom," I said. "There's a dining room in the hotel, unless you have another preference—Brown Derby, Frascati's, something like that."

"Oh no—" she said, "I mean, the hotel would be fine. But you don't have to feed me. I mean, I don't want just to be on your hands—I guess I don't know what I mean."

"You're cute when you get fussed," I said. "Keeps you honest. Excuse me, I'll wash up."

She watched with that half-scared, half-expectant look while I moved away to the bathroom.

* * * *

The hotel dining room had been built forty years before and they had remodeled it to modern by certain makeshift devices, but the service was good, the prices right and a trio played quietly in the corner.

We weren't very talkative. Nothing at all was said about the recent past. With one and a half proper drinks under her belt, Alice's face took on color and animation. I found she could laugh without restraint at something that struck her truly funny—or "amusing," as she would have called it. We got so animated, in fact, that I broke down and ordered the bottle of champagne I'd joked about up in the room. It was chilled at about the time we finished our steaks and we used it in place of coffee. Alice giggled when the cork popped.

We raised our glasses.

"To people everywhere," she said, "who ever toiled in Julie Porter's vineyard."

We drank to it, then to other things—silly things. Alice's nose wrinkled at every sip.

"I'm very fond of champagne really," she said. "I don't know why it makes me do such silly things."

But even when she tried, she couldn't help wrinkling her nose. She was working on the problem furiously when a boy wandered through the room, paging someone with a Scotch name. He repeated it three or four times and Alice suddenly said, "That's you!"

"So it is," I said. "Excuse me. If you have to be a pig with the champagne, order another bottle in time."

She wrinkled her nose at me.

The boy took me to a row of house phones behind a planter and I picked one up and gave the operator my name. I waited a few seconds and a man's voice spoke—Julie Porter's voice. "Mac—they got Linda—!"

"Hold it," I said, "and hang up. I'll call right back."

I hung up loudly to give him the idea and went around the planter at a trot. There were three phone booths in a gloomy corner. None was in use. I dived into the nearest one, found Julie's number in my pocket and dialed it. He picked it up in the middle of the first ring.

"All right," I said. "No switchboard now. Go ahead."

"Listen, boy—she was out playing. An hour ago, still daylight. Sophie was watching her, I was watching her—I don't know—Sophie called her, she didn't come, we started looking—anyway, she was gone. Ten minutes ago I got a phone call."

"What was the message?"

"Some guy—some son of a bitch—he said drive to the military dump off San Fernando Road in Glendale. Around on the back road and drop off twenty thousand dollars wrapped in foil and—"

"Wait a minute. Have you got the money?"

"Yeah. I brought it home after that second letter."

"Did he say anything about Linda?"

"He said—" there was some sound as of a throat clearing—"he said she was all right."

"Did he say where you could find her?"

"No."

"Or that she would be brought home?"

"He said she was all right and I would see her soon."

"Didn't Sophie notice anything? Hear anything?"

"Sophie's hysterical. I called a doctor."

"Try to remember if she said anything, Julie. Everything's important."

"No—Christ, she couldn't talk even. Look, Mac—what the hell will I do? I can't sit here—"

"All right, Julie. What about the police?"

"No! I mean, what the hell good—"

"Look, I'll help, one way or the other, but you have to decide."

"I'm afraid, Mac, if they let the word out—reporters, TV, all that—Jesus."

"So?"

"No cops. No nothing! Everybody ran out on me—that goddam governess—"

"Easy, boy," I said. "Have you heard from Carol?"

"No."

"Or Gen?"

"No."

"When will the doctor get there for Sophie?"

"Any minute."

"Anybody else in the house?"

"No. I called that Walewski—the guy should show up—"

"All right, here's what to do. Ask the doctor to give Sophie a strong sedative. When Walewski gets there, tell him Linda is spending the night with friends; that Sophie is sick; that you have to go out and you want someone to keep an eye on the place."

"That sounds phony even to me."

"He has to believe you. Don't worry about that."

"Okay, what else?"

"Wrap up the money, as the caller told you. Do everything exactly the way he told you. Better not use the phone again, he may be watching. When the doctor shows up, leave the door open, tell him in a loud voice you don't know what got into Sophie, she's upstairs and so on. Say it loud, so if the bastard is listening around, he'll know you're not mentioning Linda. Do the same with Walewski."

"Okay."

"How long a drive is it for you to this place?"

"Forty-five minutes."

"And from here—downtown?"

"Oh—twenty minutes."

"Then you can start any time. Don't use your own car. Can you grab another?"

"Sure, I'll rent one."

"Whatever you think. But get a different make, one that won't be spotted."

"Okay."

"Now listen—I'll be there ahead of you. You won't see me. When you plant the money, if he's not following you too close, I'll climb in with you. But he may be riding your back. In that case—you with me—?"

"Yeah, go ahead."

"In that case, plant the money and keep going to the first turn that will bring you around again. Pick up speed after you turn and get back fast. I'll be in sight."

"Why can't I ditch the car and we grab him on the spot?"

"If Linda is with him," I said, "I'll tackle him. If she isn't, and he has an accomplice somewhere—" I didn't have to say more.

"Yeah, Mac."

"You got it all, Julie?"

"I got it."

"All right. Try not to panic. I'll be there."

"Right, boy."

He hung up. When I got out of the booth my face was dripping; I mopped it dry and went back to the dining room. Alice smiled, then cut it off and came up out of her chair. "What is it?"

I reached for her arm. "Something has come up. Let's go up to the room."

She came along without question. It was a good thing, because my throat wasn't in talking condition.

In the room, I urged her into a chair, a little roughly, and got out of my coat. I found my gun in the suitcase, strapped it on and put the coat on over it. Alice eyed me silently.

"I'd like you to stay right here," I said. "Make yourself at home. I'll be back as soon as possible."

"What is it, Mac? Please?"

I shaped my hat and got it on.

"Somebody grabbed Linda," I said.

"Oh, no!" It was a low moan. "Oh, God, no—it can't be—"

"Yeah. I have to go—"

She was on her feet. "I'm going with you—"

"No, stay here."

"I can't—"

"You'll have to."

"Oh, God," she said.

"If you can pray, so much the better."

"I'll try, Mac. Find her—please—"

"I'll call you. If anyone calls here, tell the operator I'm out."

"All right."

I had the door open. "Better bolt this," I said. "Don't open to anyone. You'll be safe. If you have to say anything, say you're my secretary."

CHAPTER SIXTEEN

My cab driver was quiet and competent. When I told him my destination, he nodded and got away, easing smoothly into the downtown traffic. After a couple of blocks, he said, "Yeah, I know where it is."

I had the feeling he really knew. If it seemed an odd place for a fare to head for at this hour, he didn't appear to care.

He worked rapidly away from the civic center and onto the Hollywood Freeway, but turned off at the interchange. We dipped under a sign reading, "Arroyo Seco," and "Pasadena." Then after a couple of miles, he turned off again at a numbered avenue heading into Glendale. We drove through quiet streets past old frame houses, neighborhood shopping centers, taverns with the names of popular beers in neon. Off to the left was a sprawling industrial area, largely dark. A short freight train rumbled past.

The houses thinned and chopped away behind us. We traveled a dingy, wide, empty thoroughfare between the railroad on the left and the fenced yards of factories and warehouses on our right. Here and there a night shift worked, but most of the buildings were dark. Street intersections were few and far between.

The driver slowed and I looked at my watch. It had been fourteen minutes since I'd left the hotel. Julie would be en route by now.

And who else, and where, and how far behind?

The corner of a ten-foot steel wire fence loomed at a dark intersection. It stretched out of sight in both directions, apparently enclosing a huge dump or storage lot. Beyond the fence I could make out vague shapes like tractors, bulldozers, possibly military tanks.

"This is it," the driver said. "You want to go up this side or the other one?"

"How far to the other side?"

"Quarter mile, more or less."

"Let's go on up there."

Midway along the huge lot was a gate in the high fence. I could see the stored shapes more clearly now. They were military vehicles. One corner appeared reserved for a small ammunition dump.

At the next service road, dead-ending at this through street, like the previous one at which we had paused, a white metal sign read: "U.S. Government—Military Reservation. No Trespassing."

"This a government road?" I asked the driver.

"No—only the dump there. Road's county. The government probably paid for it."

He made his turn carefully.

The road was dark, straight and well maintained. It ran between two fences—the high, federal one on the right and a lower, evidently private one on our left. On each side, the weeds had been trimmed down. There were gravel shoulders and no ditches. No place to hide. In the sweep of the cab's headlights, I could see clearly from fence to fence, seventy or eighty feet ahead. The kidnaper had picked his spot well. The U-shaped service road surrounding the dump was clear, untraveled at night, and with access only at points where it would be impossible for a car to lurk in hiding, or even a motorcycle for that matter. The slightest suspicion of any snooping or ambush would be enough to send him on his way, leaving the ransom untouched and nobody the wiser.

I thought about Linda briefly, then thrust the images aside. The picture of that pale face, the intense olive-shaped eyes, framed by the lustrous black hair—the idea of this in pain, under threat of attack, distorted my senses. I would have to take first things first.

The driver had slowed, was looking back over his shoulder. "So you want to go around, make the loop or what?"

"Make the turn anyway," I said. "I'll see."

We began another slow right turn, heading down the back end of the lot. Only now on the left there was no fence and no maintenance. A slope of wasteland rose to maybe twenty-five feet, then leveled off. Beyond was the vague glow of city night light. There were no trees on the slope, only some sparse brush in clumps here and there. Far down at the end of the lot was a row of tall trees ranging back up the low hill.

In the center of the back fence, as in the other two sections we had passed, was another wide gate, closed and locked. Across the road, opposite, stood a lone wooden post, six feet high and slightly askew. I could see no reason for its existence, except that possibly there had once been a wooden fence on that side of the road and this post was the lone survivor. It leaned at just enough angle to make me squeamish and our headlights gleamed momentarily on a couple of protruding rusty nails.

We went on thirty feet beyond the post and I asked the driver to stop. "This'll do," I said. "I'll get out here."

He looked both ways and turned slowly to look at me. "Right here?" he said.

I climbed out. With some deliberation he pulled down the lever on his meter and tore off the tab. I brought up money.

"All right," he said, "but if you're thinking of knocking over this government warehouse, take it from me—" I shook my head, handed him the fare and a five-dollar tip. He picked up his routing board and pencil, hesitated and looked out at me. "Any reason I shouldn't mark this down exactly?" he said.

"No," I said. "When do you turn it in?"

"When I go in. Six, seven o'clock in the morning."

"Okay," I said.

He filled in his report, dropped the board and went into gear. "You want me to come back, pick you up?"

I shook my head. "No, thanks." I managed a faint leer. "I'm meeting a friend. We have to be kind of careful."

He nodded wisely. I don't know what message he got, but it must have been the right one because nothing ever came of it. I watched his taillights fade, halt and swing out of sight, and in a moment of blind panic, with Linda's white face before me like a dream, had to restrain myself from running after him. I managed to dis-invoke Linda's image, but the fear remained, a hard lump in my belly. I wished I had persuaded Julie to call the police.

I walked back to the crooked post, as if drawn to it. I looked it over and it was nothing but an old post, dry and dusty, with a couple of bent nails sticking out of it. I studied the slope for a place to hide, preferably at this midpoint, so I could see the stretch of the back road from end to end.

I began to climb carefully, scattering dirt and pebbles under my feet, slipping now and then. From the road, some of the brush clumps had appeared sizable, but when I reached them, they had dwindled and looked too skimpy for adequate cover.

I knew from observation that by going all the way up and dropping beyond the brow of the slope, I would be invisible from the road, but it seemed too far away. Still, the higher I climbed, the less choice I seemed to have. I tested two or three of the lower bushes, squatting or lying behind them in this position or that, but each time too much of me showed around the edges. I could have managed in the dark, but it was too risky with headlights involved, and possibly a spotlight. The bushes had a high aroma, dry and pungent. Sagebrush, I guessed. From one of them I flushed a litter of field mice and my stomach convulsed as they ran across my hands.

Whether I wanted to or not, I gained the top of the rise and looked down over the storage lot and dump and the bordering roads. From this height, the ranked equipment took on more definite shape. Directly below I could see the old, leaning post plainly and, across from it, the gate. The whole stretch of the road was clear and I could see a short section at either end where the turns formed the bottom corners of the U-shaped approach off the through street. Occasionally headlamps flashed distantly.

Beyond the ridge-like crest, the hill fell steeply into a ravine with what looked like a river wash at the bottom. Across it, a mile away, there were lights and far off to the right the ribbon-like freeway. I moved along the ridge to a clump of sagebrush and dug with my heel in the soft ground. As I settled down in the hollow behind the bush, I turned my coat collar up. On the other side of the hill it had been warm, but some quirk of contour changed the climate here and a cold draft swept up from the ravine. I hunched down and wondered whether I had other cause to be cold.

What if I miss him? I thought. What if I came to the wrong place? What if Julie got it wrong? Or if Julie should break down, get some wild hunch— Then Linda's face came again and it took a long time to get rid of it.

…that day we went to the ice-cream parlor…the big-shot way she turned up at school with a male escort…the clean, little-girl line of her diving into the pool…and the voice, the bell-like voice playing grown-up with the grown-up words…

Panic changed to fury. One hair on that head, I promised in a welter of bloody images. I'll settle it Julie's way—I knew what he felt then. Give the poor bastard a break, sure. Let him run.

…I saw him running, stumbling when I shot his legs out from under him…picking him up, making him stand on them, faceless under my hands beating him down again…

Slowly I pushed the picture away, scrounged deeper into the scooped-out hillside, looked at the empty road and waited.

* * * *

The tips of my fingers went raw, digging into the gravel. Minute by minute I had to make myself lift my own hands, flex and loosen them. A minute later they were digging again. I watched the light flashes from unseen traffic on the through street, rising, holding and fading as each car or truck approaching the dump passed it and went on. I settled on the two points where, by projection of either arm of the U-shaped turnoff, I could tell by the glare and angle of the light whether it was turning toward me or going on. Then I swiveled my eyes continually back and forth between the points. It didn't mean too much but it gave me something to do—something besides digging foxholes with my hands and dreaming nightmares about Linda.

As waiting goes by the clock, it wasn't very long. I counted every brace of lights that passed, then finally gave it up as idle and lulling. Within three or four minutes from the time I stopped the counting, it happened.

The light approached from my right, more slowly than the normal pace of the traffic. I watched it grow, slowing, the glare brightening as it neared the crucial point, and pausing, hovering for a split second. Then it swung in a wide bright arc into the turn. The black shapes of trucks and tanks in the storage lot faded to a distinguishable gray as the light moved slowly toward the back road. I dug in with hands and knees behind my brush screen, like a runner under the starting gun. The light paused again, then swung into the road below, sweeping the slope as it turned, and I saw the gleaming, expensive hood of a late model, heavy car, light in color. It nosed into the straightaway and drifted forward slowly. The lower edge of my vision followed it. It stopped directly below me, at that old fence post. No light had shown on the street that could be considered a tail on it. I looked directly at the post, thirty feet down the hill from where I crouched.

Julie was leaning out the window, reaching toward the post. I saw a glint of silver in his hands. He was attaching it to the post, probably hanging it on one of the nails. It meant the quarry wouldn't be too far behind. He couldn't risk leaving the money hanging in plain sight on a public road. He could wait an hour—or maybe a couple of minutes. There was still no sign of his approach. I stood up behind the bush. Julie finished his task and withdrew into the car. His motor raced quietly. I started down, trying to watch Julie, the distant street and my own path all at once.

Two-thirds of the way down, I stumbled, failed to catch myself, fell heavily on my side.

"Julie—!"

I heard the thud of his brake. I rolled down, gaining speed, trying to catch loose gravel with my hands and heels. A few feet from the post, I got some traction and slid to a stop on one hip.

He had the rear door open and I crawled in on the floor of the back seat. The door closed.

"Mac—" he growled.

"All right," I said. "Go ahead very slow. There's a chance—at the end up there, there's a row of trees. If there's space enough, we can stake out behind them—if they're thick enough."

"Yeah," he said.

I crouched on the floor, getting my breath, brushing at the clinging debris from the hillside. After a few seconds I raised up enough to scout through the back window. Still no sign of our boy. The floor of the big car vibrated under my knees as Julie drove slowly toward the end of the road.

* * * *

We got our first solid break. Not only did the trees form a thick screen, there was also a board fence, old but opaque. The space beyond it was rough, rock-strewn.

"Can you get into it," I asked Julie, "without breaking anything?"

"Hell with the breakage—"

"But we have to be able to go," I said.

"Stinking bulldozer will go anywhere."

His breathing was heavy, shallow. There was an odor of tension about him.

"All right," I said, "But slow, Julie."

He had swung into the side road leading back to the street, prepared to back into the drop. He pushed the wrong button on his automatic panel and the car bucked. He cursed under his breath and got it into reverse.

"Easy," I said.

I knelt on the back seat to check his directions. He got it straightened out with some space between us and the old fence.

"Turn off the lights," I said. "Straight back."

The lights went out. He struck a big rock and the tire squeaked. Julie swore.

"Go ahead," I said. "Get well back of the end of the fence."

He pushed it back. I climbed out of the car and walked along the fence toward the road. I signaled him to go on back and he did it. He cleared the end of the fence and I stopped him. I looked around the fence and down the road. I could see the glint of the foil-wrapped package on the black post.

I returned to the car and got in beside Julie, my head back against the seat. It ached and inside my nose it felt loose and disorganized. I couldn't breathe freely. I wondered if I had broken it rolling down the hill, but it didn't feel broken. Julie fumbled in his coat, came up with cigarettes.

"I wouldn't smoke, Julie," I said. "If he comes, he'll be all eyes."

"How long do we give him?"

"An hour, maybe two."

"If he doesn't show up—?"

"We call the police."

His big hands clenched on the wheel. "Jesus," he said softly.

It would be easier on both of us, I thought, if I could keep him talking. "Did he tell you to hang the payoff on the post?" I asked.

"Yeah."

"He set it up pretty carefully."

"The son of a bitch," Julie said.

"You couldn't tell anything about his voice?"

"No. It was muffled, like he had a mouthful of something." Mechanically he reached for the cigarettes again, put them away. "I don't know—why can't we just grab him right here?" he said.

"Because, Julie—before I knew about the post, I figured if I see Linda with him in the car and if he had to get out of the car to pick up the money, then I could brace him. Fine. But he won't have to get out of the car. If Linda is with him, it would be too risky to jump him in the car—risky for Linda."

"But if she isn't with him—we grab him, hang him up somewhere and find out—"

"Julie," I said, "this isn't a movie. This is real, remember? We maybe couldn't see Linda in the car. But even if we knew she wasn't with him, we couldn't take the chance. If he has an accomplice, somewhere else with Linda, with a set of instructions based on when this bastard returns, say, and if he doesn't get there on time—"

Julie put his head on the wheel and rubbed it hard against the corrugated rim. "Okay, okay. We let him think he's getting away with it—"

"Till we find Linda," I said.

Talking about her had brought the bad dream again. I felt those constrictions in my neck and jaw, like hot wires drawing steadily tighter. It impaired my hearing. I had to ask Julie to repeat himself.

"I said—when we find her—will you let me have him?"

Somebody gave the wires another twist.

"I'll race you for him," I said.

So we waited.

CHAPTER SEVENTEEN

When he finally came, it caught me off guard. I had run another gauntlet of fear and fury and I don't know what had gone through Julie's mind, as to details. This bout had left me in a sweat and I was wiping it off with my sleeve when Julie grunted, "Look!"

I blinked and saw the light, an expanding gray glow on the road to our right. My hands began to shake.

Christ, I thought, what if he had come in the other way, straight at us? What made me think he'd come that other way? How many mistakes can a man make—The light grew, lengthening along the road. I could see it gleam on the strands of wire in the high fence and a silver highlight along the edge of the fence ahead and to our right. The light stopped, holding on these things. I pictured an arm reaching out to snag the foil package, tried, by counting, to estimate the time it would take. Julie had leaned forward, his hand fumbling at the starter button. I grabbed his sleeve.

"Don't start it till he's made the turn going away," I said. "We spook him now and it would be murder."

But what if he had come in this other way, I thought, and seen us waiting here? It would have been murder then all right.

"If he goes out this way," Julie said, "he'll see us in the rear view. Even in the dark—"

"Maybe not," I said. "We'll get down. If he sees the car at all, it's just sitting here—maybe junk—maybe a necking party. We wait till he turns onto the street."

"What if we lose him?"

"We won't lose him."

The light moved, paused, came on, widening and brightening.

"Get down," I said, ducking below the dash.

"I want to get a look—" I grabbed his shoulder, yanking.

"Down, goddam it!" He came down. I could feel his breath hot on my neck. The light increased, glaring around us. I heard my heart thumping, positive he had swung toward us, was watching. Then it shifted abruptly, started away. I could hear his motor now.

Julie started up and I held him for a count of three, then let go and we both looked.

It was a light-colored, hardtop convertible, going away not too fast.

"Start it," I said. "No lights."

The big car rumbled to life. Ahead, the convertible reached the street, paused, swung slowly into a right turn.

"Go, for God's sake!" I said.

We went down the dark road, hitting fifty-five at the midway gate.

"Easy," I shouted.

He slowed some and made a sensible approach to the turn. A truck bore down from our left, barreling, and Julie cursed.

"Good," I said. "Get behind him. Not too close."

The trucker was heading for somewhere and evidently knew he wouldn't tangle with much cross traffic. His motor roared and he blinked his lights at something in his path, then began the swing out to go around it. I touched Julie's arm.

"Don't go with him. Stay back."

Allowing for the long truck, our distance behind and a respectable clearance ahead, there was a minimum seventy-five yards between us and our subject in the hardtop convertible—if he was still there at all. For about two minutes we had no way to tell. The truck lights flashed again, front and back, and he roared out to the left, spraying gravel at us. As he cleared a channel directly ahead I saw there was a car up there all right, but the glare of the truck lights distorted it, made it unrecognizable. It was at least eighty yards in front and not slackening any for the passing truck.

"Is it him?" Julie yelled.

"I don't know!"

For a few seconds the truck and the car ran abreast and it was nip and tuck as to which would take the lead. Julie began sneaking up in our own lane and I let him pick up twenty or thirty yards, then waved him down again. He made a sound of exasperation. I didn't blame him for a second, but I had been through this before, though never on such an errand.

In the race for leadership, the truck began to pull ahead. As its flashing lights moved on, the car in front of us took on a more normal shape and color. But I still couldn't read the license plate and urged Julie to take up more of the slack. He was willing. I sat forward, peering at the dimly lighted frame around the plate.

"Boy, if that isn't him—" Julie growled.

"It's him," I said.

I sat back in the seat. Julie blew out some breath violently.

"The thing to watch for," I said, "is if he stops. Don't stop with him or turn off sharp behind him. Just go on by to the first right turn, okay?"

"Okay."

We were leaving the industrial section behind, coming into another of those quiet neighborhoods of small houses, shopping centers and an occasional tavern. This section was a little higher class than that hard by the freeway. We ran into traffic signals and were staying a block behind him in the convertible.

"How's the gas?" I asked.

Julie looked at the gauge. "Jesus," he said, "he might go anywhere—Ventura, San Diego, Tijuana—"

"Hang on awhile. We'll move in if he goes too far."

After a couple of blocks, I asked, "Do you recognize the car?"

"Hell, no. All cars are alike to me."

A minute later he said, "Mac, I know there wasn't anything with you and Carol. I guess I didn't believe it even at the time. I was steamed."

"There's something about the dead past, remember?" I said.

There was that word again. *Dead.* I'd had a regular run of them tonight—*dead, murder*—"Yeah," Julie said. "Bernie's dead. Carol's gone—"

"She may come back."

"No, she won't. Would you?" Then with a savage shift, "If he did anything to Linda, by God—"

"Let's hang on, Julie."

Momentarily the car bucked under a sudden brake. I set my hand against the padded dash, ducking. We rolled on then.

"The son of a bitch stopped," Julie said.

He had stopped in the middle of the next block, in front of a lighted neighborhood tavern. His lights went out.

"Keep going," I said. "Don't look at him when we pass."

"He'll look at us."

"Maybe. Give me one of those cigarettes."

He fumbled the package out to me.

"Sit down in the seat, get shorter than me," I said.

He slid down. I found a match, got the cigarette in my mouth. We were just behind him now, in the open lane, and I saw through his back window that he was looking out toward the tavern. There was no sign of Linda in the car.

Julie swung out a little, passing, and I struck the match and cupped my hands loosely, covering my lower face. If his mind was busy enough and he hadn't got suspicious so far…

We had no choice but the risk. It took all the control I had to keep from looking at him as we passed. I managed and shook out the match. The unaccustomed cigarette was raw tasting in my mouth.

"Bear right and turn," I said. "Stop at the first possible spot."

He stepped it up a little, heading into the turn. It was a wide, dark, tree-fined street. Most of the houses were dark. There were plenty of places to pull in. Julie eased to the curb and turned the thing off. I was halfway out of the car. Julie's feet scraped the concrete, catching up. We walked fast over the grass parking to the corner. I looked around the edge of a brick building toward the tavern. My breath clogged my throat. I gestured to Julie, who looked around past me.

"Him!" he said, soft, explosive.

The guy had left the car, paused to push the door to. Then he moved across the walk toward the tavern, swinging his useless legs in long, rhythmic surges. Garwood Reilly.

CHAPTER EIGHTEEN

Julie was saying something in his throat, but I couldn't make out the words.

"When he hits the entrance—" I said. "He may be stopping for a drink—or maybe to make a phone call. We have to be there when he makes it."

Reilly reached the tavern door, paused and disappeared. I nudged Julie and we started down there at a trot past dark store-fronts. For a man of his weight and build, he was light on his feet.

"Check the car for Linda," I said, "then come on in."

"I—"

"Do it, Julie!"

He threw one desperate glance toward the tavern, then ran across the walk to the car. I heard him open it as I turned into the joint.

There was a curving passage off the street to an inset door with a small glass panel at eye level. Inside was a planter screen and another passage. I couldn't see into the bar proper.

The padded swinging door opened noiselessly and I walked in behind the planter. Through the foliage I saw the dimly lighted interior of the bar, a few booths. There were half a dozen customers, all of them on bar stools.

The door swung behind me and I looked around at Julie. He shook his head. I looked again through the planter and saw Reilly limping away from the bar toward a back corner of the room. There was a curtained archway labeled Rest Rooms. No doubt there was also a wall telephone.

With sign language, I directed Julie to the bar to order a drink. He nodded reluctantly. As we strolled around the end of the planter, Reilly was at the back curtains. I split away from Julie. After a moment I heard him order a highball.

The curtains closing the passage to the rest rooms billowed outward slightly. Through the crack between them I could see part of Reilly's back as he stood facing the wall. His right arm went up and I heard the coin click dully into the slot. I looked toward the bar, spreading my hands to show I too was waiting for the phone. Julie's big hand clenched a highball glass. When I looked at him, he raised it and poured some in his mouth. It was simple reflex. I doubted he was tasting anything or even feeling the wet of it.

Reilly was dialing and I could hear the muffled rasp of it through the curtains. I stood on one foot, then the other, with my back to the curtains, waiting. If I was also listening, the bored bartender in the white, blue-trimmed jacket seemed not to notice. Julie lifted his glass again and I held my breath, waiting for him to gag on it, but he kept it down.

Reilly was silent. He had finished the dialing and was evidently waiting for the answer. It seemed like a long time. I risked a glance through the opening between the curtains, and he was standing close to the telephone, looking at the wall. I turned away, shifting to put my ear in direct line with the instrument. Suddenly he was talking. A mutter, at first, that I couldn't understand. Then he said, "Yeah, I got it. What?..."

I glanced at Julie. He had got down from his stool and was rolling his glass slowly in his hand, staring at me. I shook my head and he looked away. The bartender banged something into the cash register, turned around and started watching me. I didn't spend any precious time watching him.

I heard Reilly say, "Quit worrying… Yeah, I'll be there in half an hour—you be ready—Okay."

I backed between the curtains, swinging to face him. The words "You be ready," had scared me, thrown my timing off. He had the mouthpiece poised over the hook, but he hadn't broken the connection yet when he saw me. He opened his mouth and I reached for his wrist and caught it in time to bang down the hook. Then I had my gun out and was crowding him against the wall beside the phone. In place of the warning shout his mouth had prepared, words came out, soft and tumbling. There was sweat on his forehead like wet flour squeezed out of a sifter.

"Listen, the kid is okay," he said, "the money's in the car. You can have it. Just give me five minutes to get out—"

"One step at a time, Reilly," I said. "First comes Linda."

"She's all right, I swear. I wouldn't have hurt her—"

"Where is she?"

It was the last ounce of bargaining material he owned and I had no way of knowing whether it was worth anything even to him.

"Just that one little break," he said. "I was crazy, I admit it, the money's in a package in the car—" I grabbed his shirt front and lifted outward, squeezing his tie around his throat. He lifted a hand feebly and I batted it aside.

"I have nothing to say about it," I said. "I'm working for Julie. Where's Linda?"

He opened his mouth, looked over my shoulder and his eyes went crooked. I felt a draft.

"No, Julie," I said, "wait a minute—" Julie made some sound—I've only heard it two or three times in my life, and each time somebody died soon after. He pushed me aside as if I were a laundry hamper and moved in, reaching for Reilly.

"No! Julie—!" the guy yelled.

Then I was trying to get out of the way. Julie was dragging Reilly out into the bar while the lame one tried to get a purchase with his dangling legs. I slid out around them into the open, keeping the gun down out of sight. The bartender and all six of the customers were staring at us.

"Hey—!" the bartender said.

He was moving behind the bar in our direction and I knew he must be heeled.

"Hold it," I said. "We won't be long."

"You can't do that—" he said.

Julie had Reilly well out now and he was growling in his throat. One of the female customers screamed.

"Julie!" I said, but he never even heard it.

"He's a cripple!" a customer said. "What the hell kind of—?"

"Cut it out!" the bartender yelled.

I brought the gun out where he could see it and he stopped talking, but his hand was snaking toward a telephone on the service bar. I moved over there. The lady who had screamed fainted and fell off her stool. A guy got down beside her.

"We're only after him," I said, jerking my head. "Just hold still."

"Hold still—" the bartender said. "In a pig's eye, goddam it—"

He paid no attention to the gun and I couldn't make any use of it. I jumped to the end of the bar, grabbed the phone and jerked the cord out of wherever it was socketed. The bartender grabbed a bottle and swung at my head and I ducked. Accidentally, I discharged my revolver and tore a gash in the asphalt tile floor. The bartender straightened up and stood still. The woman on the floor was whimpering. I glanced at the others and none of them looked very active. I turned my attention to Julie.

He had hold of Reilly's throat and was shaking him. The guy's feet scraped helplessly over the floor. He made a few feeble efforts to slap at Julie, but didn't connect.

"Julie, that's enough!" I yelled at him.

Julie still couldn't hear me. I put the gun away, lowered my head and went in between them. Julie began losing his grip and swung a wild one. I raised up and it caught me on the cheekbone. I felt the blood start. I managed to break the rest of his grip and Reilly fell heavily on the floor. I caught Julie around the waist and ran him back into one of the booths where he sprawled backward. When I turned around, the bartender was coming at me with a stick. He swung with it and I caught it in one hand, jerked him forward and got him by the lapels of his jacket.

"Listen," I said. "I'm an out-of-town cop. The guy on the floor is a kid snatcher. We don't know whether the kid is all right yet or not. I tried to make a pinch in there and the kid's father got a little upset. That's the whole story. Now get back there and leave us alone so we can get him out of here. Any damage to the bar, we'll pay for."

Three of the customers had got down and stood in a tight little group near the bar. The bartender backed off and one of them said, "Sounds offbeat to me. It's a gang thing. Go ahead, grab him. We'll back you up."

I looked at them for a moment, decided they were halfhearted and turned back to find Julie. He was puffing himself out of the booth. Reilly was rolling on the floor, massaging his neck.

"Come on," I said to Julie, "let's get out of here."

He came along, his first frenzy worked out of him. We got hold of Reilly, one by each arm and carried him to the door. In the shelter of the planter I propped him up and nudged his face till he quit squirming.

"We're going with you to wherever Linda is," I said. "One bad move and I give you back to Julie. Now let's go."

Julie shouldered the swinging door and we carried Reilly through it.

"Hurry," I said. "That bartender will send for the cops. I'll go with Reilly in his car. You follow."

"Yeah," Julie said.

He helped me get Reilly into the car and went off toward the corner. Reilly was in bad shape, but seemed to be moving well enough to drive. The thing had a hand brake and feed, and I guessed he had borrowed the car from another paraplegic.

"Get going," I told him, "to wherever you planned to go."

He looked at me with his mouth working. All I could hear was a squawk. He rolled down the window and leaned out. I heard him spitting. He came in, tried to talk again but couldn't make any words.

Julie must have crushed his larynx, I thought.

"Just get the car going," I said. "If you're trying to talk a deal, it's up to Julie. He might give you a chance. But I can say this—the only chance you've got in the world is to take us to Linda. If anything has happened to her, and if Julie doesn't kill you, I will."

He kept moving his mouth. I raised the back of my hand and he bent over the wheel and got it started. Up ahead, Julie's car eased out of a U-turn and hovered, waiting. Reilly pulled out, weaving, then got it straight and held it steady. As we passed the corner, I signaled an okay to Julie and he swung in behind us.

We drove two blocks and the car swerved violently. By the time I got to the wheel and hauled Reilly's hand off the gas feed, we were halfway to the wrong side curb. I steered it on an angle to the legal curb and stalled it.

Reilly's head was on the wheel; his hands worked at his throat. I climbed out and Julie came to meet me.

"He can't drive," I said, "and he can't talk. What did you do to him?"

"I don't know—I blew my stack—"

"We'll have to get him fixed up. We get nowhere this way."

"Fixed up—"

"Got a pencil?" I asked.

"Sure. I don't know—" He came up with a pencil. I took a notebook out of my coat, found a clean page and we went to the car again. Reilly was still slumped on the wheel. I prodded him and he looked up.

"Couple of questions," I said. "If you can't talk, you can write."

I handed him the pencil and notebook. He looked at it vaguely and shook his head.

"Look, Reilly," I said, "we're going to find Linda if we have to make a house-to-house canvass on every street in Los Angeles. And we're going to keep you conscious for every minute of it. The sooner you give out, the sooner you get to a doctor. Clear?"

He gave me that look and finally he nodded.

"Where's Linda?" I asked him.

He fumbled with the pencil, scratched at the paper. Beads of sweat stood out like pearls on his gray face. He seemed to be having great difficulty with the pencil.

"Come on!" I urged him.

Suddenly he crumpled heavily onto the wheel, tilted to one side and collapsed on the seat. The pencil and pad slipped out of sight. Julie, on the curb side, started into the car.

"Hold it," I said. "Can you find the paper?"

He groped for it on the floor, finally brought it up.

"What did he write?" I asked.

"'Holly,'" he said.

"That's all? Just 'Holly'?"

"That's all."

"Holly—wood?"

"Sure, Hollywood. It's not even a place, just an idea."

"Does he know anybody named Holly—a girl-friend?"

"I don't know."

"Where does he live?"

"Hollywood."

"You know the address?"

"No. Up in the hills—he's in the book."

"We have to start somewhere," I said.

I slid under the wheel, nudging Reilly's legs out of the way. "I'll follow you. Find a phone book, then a doctor or a small hospital—"

"Hospital! For him—?"

"If he dies, Julie, they'll have you for it."

He backed out of the doorway, closed it and disappeared. I started Reilly's car and waited for Julie to pull around in front. On the seat, Reilly was groaning, making those squawking sounds. There was the smell of blood. I found a limp wrist and a weak, sporadic pulse.

Julie pulled out from the curb and rumbled ahead and I eased into his wake. Reilly's groans were getting under my skin. I hoped Julie would waste no time finding a doctor.

I followed him for a mile through the residential area, then we hit another commercial stretch. We passed a big bakery and Julie turned left, crossing some tracks. The aroma from the bake ovens was rich and full-bodied in the warm night.

A sign read: Hollywood 6 mi. We followed a curving route around hills. Traffic was light and the signals were generously timed. We came into Sunset Boulevard on an angle and cut back toward the Hollywood lights. Julie pulled up in front of a dark shopping center. To save time, I stayed in the car, waiting. I watched him get out, go into a street-side telephone booth and raise a directory, leaf through it rapidly. He found what he wanted, dropped the thick book and returned to his car. We moved on toward the Hollywood business center. We passed a television studio, a bowling alley. Julie was setting a fast pace, illegal by ten or fifteen miles, and there was no way for me to hold him down. I tried to think of an explanation for Reilly and his condition, in case a traffic cop should haul me over. Then Julie braked sharply, made a right turn at Gower Street and the speed worry was over.

Two blocks, and Julie turned left on a narrow street, pulled up beside a low frame building with the words "Hollywood Emergency Hospital" in faded blue neon over the front entrance. It was a good, quiet, out-of-the-way selection. Julie was settling down.

I pulled in behind him, switched on the dash light and started through Reilly's pockets. Julie looked in across the seat.

"Just a minute," I said.

I went through Reilly's well-worn wallet. It contained no money. There were a couple of credit cards, a calendar, some bar and restaurant tabs, a few postage stamps. The rest of the haul out of his pockets consisted of cigarettes, matches, paper clips and a clean handkerchief. I put the wallet in his pocket along with the cigarettes.

I was looking over the car when Julie blurted, "What the hell you doing now?"

"Looking for the money," I said.

"The hell with the money."

"We'll have to leave some with him," I said. "The way I've heard it, if there's not enough money showing, they may just let him lie there."

But Julie was right. We had no time to look for the money.

I got hold of Reilly, half-raised and slid him across the seat. Julie took over, holding him till I could get around there. When we started puffing him out of the car, Reilly hung back. I think maybe he wanted to die then—it was the only chance left to him to get Julie.

Julie swore softly and leaned into him and he came out between us. His legs slid outward at an impossible angle. We lifted and carried him across the walk to a side entrance with a naked light bulb over it. Julie pounded on the door. Between us, a nearly dead weight, Reilly was working his throat, squawking.

A middle-aged woman in glasses and a white nylon uniform came to the door and looked out, then quickly threw a bolt and opened up. We pushed Reilly at her.

"This man needs help," I said. "Payment's guaranteed. We'll be back."

We let go of him and he floundered into her. She caught him expertly, eased him to the floor. Julie and I got away fast.

"Wait a minute—" she called. Then, "Doctor—?" Then, "Harry! Get down here with a stretcher!"

Crossing the walk, I banged into a curious pedestrian, gawking toward the open hospital door.

"Hey what—?" he said.

I got him back on his feet and left him. Julie was in his car.

"You got the address?" I asked.

"Yeah."

"I'll follow you."

He nodded. By the time I got behind the wheel of the other car, he was pulling away. I looked at my watch and it was thirty-five minutes from the time we had braced Reilly in the joint. He had, over the telephone, given himself half an hour to some sort of rendezvous. What was supposed to happen, I wondered, if he didn't show up on time?

With Reilly on my hands and the necessity to keep Julie under control, I had been busy enough to think one minute at a time. Now, with a breathing space ahead, the bad dreams of what could happen to Linda came back stronger than ever. This time, I couldn't shake them. Alternately, I dried the palms of my hands on my pants and wound up into the Hollywood hills behind Julie's car. The hill streets were a labyrinth of dead ends, hairpin turns, winding lanes.

Julie's car braked under a lamppost while he leaned out to read a street name. We went on slowly to a dead end with a circle turn. Julie drove half-way around and stopped, leaving space for me behind.

We looked up at a hillside house, stucco with a red tile roof. One high, heavily draped living-room window overlooked the surrounding hills. Under it, a two-car garage had been dug out of the hillside. The house was dark.

"Let's go," I said. "If there's anyone in there, he probably saw us drive up."

We climbed a short, steep flight of stone steps to an arched entry. The front door was glass, framed in oak, with a blind drawn on the inside. Julie lifted his hand to knock and I pushed him aside and tried the knob. The door was locked.

At the far end of a concrete slab porch was a flagstone walk to the rear of the house. I beckoned to Julie and we went that way, tiptoeing. It was a touch-and-go situation if Reilly's accomplice was inside with Linda; but maybe not quite so touch-and-go as if we had been the police, official and clanking.

At the side of the house overlooking the city was a French window, also locked. It was hinged to open inward and I made out the line of an old-fashioned sofa backed against it. I started on toward the rear, then thought of something and turned back to Julie.

"Go ditch your car somewhere," I said. "In case they planned to rendez-vous here and somebody shows up, he'll see only Reilly's car."

Julie nodded obediently and went away quickly. As I got around to a wooden stoop at a high back door, I heard his motor rumble to life and the light squeak of his tires, turning.

A dilapidated screen creaked as I opened it. I slid against the wooden door panel and put my ear to it, listening for a long time. There was no sound inside. The door was locked, but felt as if it would yield without too much fuss or racket. I got out a penknife and worked at it for a while and got nowhere. I was studying it for another method when Julie returned, panting softly.

"Want in?" he said.

I nodded. "I don't think there's anyone home."

"Here," he said, pushing me aside.

His big hand swallowed the doorknob. His shoulder pressed into the panel. I saw him twist and lift. There was a light splintering sound and the door swung open.

He must have learned that as a kid on the streets, I thought. He would have been a big kid.

CHAPTER NINETEEN

Stale food odors assaulted us in the small kitchen. I found a light and we saw that everything was neat and in place. Only the odors remained of whatever had been the last meal. At the swinging door that would lead to the rest of the house, I stopped Julie again.

"We'll separate and go through fast, looking just for people," I said. "Watch your step. We'll meet back here, on the other side of the door."

I pushed through, found another light switch and we were in a dining area opening into a larger living room with the one big, shaded window. A half-open door opposite led into some sort of den. That would be where I had seen the sofa against the French window.

"Take the living room and bedrooms," I said to Julie. "I'll go in here and find the cellar—if there is one."

Julie went off into the living room. I opened the den door slowly, looked into the gloom, then moved in and found a light. There was a desk in the corner, a couple of chairs and the sofa. That was all I cared about this trip. A door in one wall opened on a small coat closet. I looked in there and found nobody. Distantly I could hear Julie tramping through other rooms, opening and closing doors.

I went back through the dining room and kitchen to the service porch and found a cellar door opening on a down-ward flight of half a dozen steps. Heat flowed up at me softly. There was no light. I found a match and lit my way down the steps, stooping to avoid the ceiling beams. Down below there was a dirt floor, a gas furnace, a hot water heater. The whole space was maybe twelve feet square. I made the circuit, lighting my way with matches. There was the strong odor of damp earth and gas, and nothing else of any interest.

When I got back to the kitchen, Julie was waiting for me at the door. He shook his head. "Nobody," he said.

"All right, let's take it apart," I said. "Keep your ear out for a car or footsteps outside."

"What're we looking for?"

"Any clue. Anything at all. Letters, notes, telephone numbers—any goddam thing, any sign of any kind that Linda was ever in the house."

I took a moment to look at him. His face was the color of ashes. That smell was noticeable again, the smell of fear and of loss. He was looking for the one thing in his life he had ever loved wholly without stint. He had to find her or it would kill him. I could see it beginning to kill him already and no man deserves that kind of death.

"Have you ever been in this house before?" I asked him.

"No," he said.

"Go slow. Force yourself. Look at everything. Anything looks familiar, tell me about it."

He rubbed his palms together, dried them on his jacket and nodded vaguely. We went into the living room. Newspapers were scattered on a coffee table. They were the next day's edition, open to the amusements section. I lifted and looked under them. There were two envelopes addressed to Garwood Reilly. One from the gas company, another from the telephone company. Neither had been opened. They were dated three days previously. There were several water and glass ring stains on the wooden table top.

We pulled the cushions out of the chairs and a long, modern sofa and found a few paper clips, a button and a couple of pennies. I rolled back the rugs and there was nothing under them but dust.

There were two bedrooms with a connecting bath. The nearer, smaller one was clean, sparsely furnished, bare and neat with a military neatness, the bed tautly made with a carefully folded army blanket at the foot and no fancy spread. I lifted the pillow, pulled back the top covers and looked through them carefully while Julie went through the dresser drawers. We finished at the same time, looked at each other and looked away.

The bathroom was more cluttered than the bedroom, but clean on the surface. I let Julie go on to the second bedroom, then looked around for signs of a struggle, for hairs or bloodstains. There weren't any.

The other bedroom was on the frilly side, feminine and casually furnished.

"Did he go for the girls?" I asked.

"Sure," Julie said.

"If he consorted with a lot of broads, it might be any one of them in on it with him. You ever meet any of them?"

"Hell no. How would I?"

"Just keep thinking, Julie."

We were going through the bureau, dressing table, a double bed covered with a satin spread. When I opened the bed, the sheets were slightly mussed. I sniffed at them and there was the faint fragrance of powder and toilet water. On one pillow I found two long, blond hairs—blond or gray.

I started out of the room and he grabbed me, spun me around. His face was a tragic mask. "Talk to me, boy!" he roared.

"I'm going to call the police," I said.

He held onto me, his hands clenched on my shoulder pads. "No—wait—"

"Listen, Julie, we're licked. We know where Reilly is. We've got no idea in the world where Linda is. We need help!"

"But if it's that tight—the cops will blow it!"

"Maybe not. They're professionals."

"If they know what we've done so far, they'll flip. They'll get steamed and they won't think good. Some reporter will get onto it—"

I shouted back at him, twisting to get out from under his hands. "We've got no choice, Julie!"

He released me. "Maybe one," he said. "I know a guy in the Hollywood station, good boy, good cop. Worked with me on a picture. He'll handle it. We'll drive down there and tell him. Only about five minutes—"

"The phone would take about thirty seconds—"

"I'm afraid, Mac."

"So am I. We'll do it your way."

We raced each other for the front door. I won. I was at the bottom of the stone steps when I stopped and Julie piled up against me.

"That newspaper in the living room," I said. "Tomorrow's *Times.* When does it hit the street?"

"Times—? Six o'clock, six-thirty, why?"

"It was open to the amusements. I saw the list of theaters with their current bills."

"So—?"

"We know Reilly wasn't planning to go to the movies."

His hands shook in my face. "Come *on* with it!"

"If they needed a place to meet—some quiet, dark place—" Julie started back up the stairs. At the door we remembered having pulled it to, locking ourselves out. Julie raised his foot and kicked out one of the square glass panels. I reached through, found the latch and let us in. We stood over the coffee table, looking down at the open paper.

"No," Julie said dismally. "Linda won't go to the movies. She hates them. She'd raise a hell of a rumpus if somebody tried to get her into a—" He had leaned close over the paper, peering at the listings. His brow furrowed. "Except—" he murmured.

"Except what?"

He straightened sharply, lifting the page to his eyes. "Walt Disney!" he said. "She loves Walt Disney! Sometimes at her school they show a Disney—" His eyes scanned the sheet at close range. "Hollyridge Theater!" he shouted suddenly. "That's it! That's what Reilly started to put on the paper. They got a Disney picture—come on, boy!"

When I caught up with him, he was running down the middle of the narrow, hillside street, the newspaper clutched in one hand, his steps long and driving on the echoing pavement.

CHAPTER TWENTY

We careened down out of the hills. Julie never made a wrong turn. We came down Beachwood Drive at fifty-five, swung crazily into Franklin Avenue and headed west, parallel to Hollywood Boulevard. After a few blocks we twisted again and came out on a narrow street with a Spanish name. Julie handled the big car like a surgeon handles a scalpel, knifing his way through the tangled viscera of the overgrown village. He made a left turn and there was an auto park sign, red and pink over a half-filled lot. Julie swung into it and got out, leaving the door open and the motor rumbling. An attendant started over.

"Park it!" Julie yelled.

"Okay, buddy," the guy muttered, "don't get your ass—" Then we were running down the side street toward the Boulevard and the lights of a bright marquee. "Walt Disney's—"

Some tires screeched. A voice yelled from a car window. We cut diagonally across the lane of oncoming traffic and got to the curb. Half a dozen pedestrians changed course as we pounded in under the marquee. A box-office blonde in fancy glasses gave us a startled look.

There was a deep, outdoor foyer, patio style, between the box office and the entrance. A handful of showgoers drifted out of the theater proper. A man in a tuxedo strolled out behind them, leaving a half-door open. When he caught sight of Julie running toward the inner lobby, he headed back. Julie made a pushing gesture without touching him.

"Hey, wait a minute!" the guy yelled.

I blocked him out as Julie pushed inside, scattering another handful of customers. The theater managers face was close to mine.

"You can't do this—"

"We'll settle up," I said and pushed him out of the way to follow Julie. I heard the manager barking something about "Police!"

Julie's bulk was framed in one of four arched entries into the theater. I moved into the next one and looked at silhouetted heads against the lighted screen. The house was about a third full.

Julie's voice exploded in the darkened room.

"Linda! Baby!"

There was a grumble of hissed warning. Heads turned.

"Linda!" he yelled again.

I saw the theater manager and another fellow lay hands on him. Julie shrugged them off and started down the aisle. I moved with him in the next aisle. A few people got up, muttering, and started out. Julie yelled again. Someone yelled back, "Shut up!" More people rose in disgust, jamming Julie's aisle. I watched him. If he should start pushing hard and build a riot, we'd be in it good. My own aisle was clear and I started along an empty row of seats to join Julie. Somebody barked at me to sit down.

I was midway between the aisles, when it came—sleepily at first, then up, high and clear, the bell-like voice ringing: "Julie—? Daddy! Here I am, Julie!"

I stopped where I was. Her call had stopped the surge in Julie's aisle. People began moving out quietly. Then I could see her, far down in front, tiny and rigid, clinging with one hand to the back of a seat, gazing up the aisle, looking for him. Her face was a gray oval framed in the black hair.

"Julie—?" she called.

She saw him. With one of those jet-propelled take-offs, she flew up the aisle to meet him. Julie bore down with long strides, reaching to scoop her up. Behind him, two uniformed cops stalked down the aisle, clanking.

Julie would handle them. I had other business. Down near the screen, a woman had risen and was moving quickly along the front row of seats toward the exit alcove. I moved to head her off. She must have caught sight of me, because she quickened her pace, angling down toward the exit. She slid between curtains and disappeared and I ran the last few steps. There were two shallow steps and a landing with a steel door and bar-spring handle. She had the door partly open. She looked at me over her shoulder and skittered outside.

The areaway between the theater and the next building was narrow. It opened on the street at one end, a parking lot at the other. She was going fast toward the parking lot.

"Louise—" I said quietly. "It's Mac."

Her stride broke. She faltered, put out a hand to the rough plaster of the building wall. I waited, half a dozen strides behind her. She let go of the wall and half turned. I saw her fumbling at her purse, as if for a handkerchief. I took a step toward her, forming some quiet words. She turned to face me and her hand came out of the purse with a gun. I flattened against the wall, facing it, and threw my arms up to cover my face and head.

She fired point blank. I heard the crack of the firing and a dull splat against the plaster. Something cut sharply into my cheekbone. I didn't dare look at her. If she was that desperate, she might well empty the gun. Anything in the head would kill me. Anywhere else, I would have a chance.

After a thousand years, I heard a small choking sound, then her footsteps, light and irregular, going away. I lowered one arm and saw her going, carrying the gun loosely at one side. I went after her on tiptoe, hugging the wall. Half a step behind, I caught her forearms, held them tight at her sides, turning her into the wall. She writhed, her cheek pressing the plaster.

"No—please—!" she said.

"Drop the gun!" I said.

I heard it drop and relaxed my hold. She swung on me with the purse, but the strap broke and stuff spilled out of it. I caught her arms again and backed her against the wall. She looked into my face. She was nearly as tall as I was. "What did you do to Garwood?" she said, panting.

"Not much. He's in the hospital."

"Listen, he didn't do anything—"

"He picked up the money."

"But that's all! He didn't—it was me—the whole thing—"

"I know," I said. "And Bernie, too, wasn't it?"

She struggled briefly and I let go of her. She started away, then stopped, leaning against the wall, her face in her hand.

"I know what happened," I said. "That night after the preview, when Bernie asked you to call him the next morning, before you went to Tahoe… It was a matter of some importance, wasn't it?"

She was sobbing painfully.

"All right," she said. "Yes. But I wouldn't have—but he found the stamp outfit in my room. He took it with him. I went to his house and he showed me he had it. I only wanted to scare him. I knew about him and Carol—"

"There wasn't anything between Bernie and Carol, and it was a mistake to try and deal with him. Bernie had guts."

"I know." Getting rid of it, regurgitating the memories, was helping her. She straightened up against the wall and looked at me openly. "He was sitting there in that chair, just sitting—he had the stamp outfit in his hands. There was a drawer open in that table beside his chair—I saw the gun in it. The idea came like a flash. He had the stamp outfit—they would think he had tried to get money out of Julie and then had killed himself. With Bernie out of the way, Garwood would get his job—Garwood could handle that job…"

She drew a long, sighing breath. I steadied her with a hand on her arm.

"I got hold of the gun," she said. "He sat there looking up at me, shaking his head.

"'Don't do it, Louise!' he said. He didn't beg, or cry or squirm. He just kept saying, 'Don't do it,' with a sad look on his face. I shot him in the head. He twisted in the chair and put his head down. He didn't make a sound."

She looked around vaguely.

"Don't bother with the details," I said. "You set it up all right—except that you can't fool police by putting a gun in a dead man's hand. It can't be done."

She nodded.

"It was Carol who really crossed you up," I said. "She found Bernie, and the stamp outfit. She didn't want it to look that way for Bernie. She took the thing away with her."

She nodded some more. Her face was twisted to one side. "When Garwood called me and said they hadn't found the stamp outfit, I knew it was only a matter of time. If only Julie had given Garwood the job—we wouldn't have had to do the thing with Linda—"

"Wouldn't have had to?"

"We had to get away!" she said earnestly. "We needed money. That's all we ever wanted—just money, or something coming in. Nobody understands."

She shook her head savagely. I could hear it thudding against the wall. She didn't seem to notice.

"Garwood didn't have anything to do with it," she said. "Just me. I told him what to say over the phone—to Julie. I drove past the house and Linda was playing in the yard. I asked if she wanted to go for a ride. That's all. I wouldn't have hurt her—but Garwood didn't do anything wrong, not really—"

I took her arm firmly, urging her away from the wall. "All right," I said. "Let's go."

She came along for a few steps, then stopped, pulling back hard against my hand.

"Please—before—let me see Garwood, please—"

"You wouldn't want to see him now," I said. "He's probably sleeping."

"I don't care. He's my son! Don't you have any feeling at all—?"

From the Boulevard came the sound of heavy steps, a faint jingling. Louise twisted out of my grip, stumbled and fell against the wall. When I leaned to help her up, she fought me, flailing at my head with her arms. A young patrolman walked between us.

"Break it up," he said.

She went on struggling and I helped him get her subdued and under control. When she gave up, it was completely, into a stolid silence. I think at first the patrolman had taken me for another cop.

"Thanks," he said. "You all right?"

"Yeah," I said. "You'd better take her in. I'll come in and sign—whatever it takes."

Then he wasn't sure about me. "Oh?" he said. "What charge?"

I looked at Louise and she was staring at the wall.

"Kidnapping," I said, "and extortion and murder. The name is Reilly."

He blinked at me. "Your name?" he said.

"No, her name."

"Well, what's your name?"

But I was walking away then and preparing to spit and one thing and another. I stepped into a dark doorway and took time to sponge some of the blood off my face. The young cop had his hands full with Louise and he didn't waste any effort looking for me.

CHAPTER TWENTY-ONE

There was a small crowd around the outer entrance to the theater. It included half a dozen cops, two in plain clothes. The one who had taken Louise in tow was getting her into the back seat of a black-and-white prowl car. Center point of interest was Julie Porter. He had Linda in his arms, holding her high as if to keep her out of anyone's reach, and she was clinging with both arms to his neck. There was a babble of voices.

Julie strode into the clear and a couple of the cops began to disperse the crowd. One of the plain-clothes men heeled Julie like a faithful dog. I moved across the walk to join them. Julie's face questioned me and I nodded.

"Just a minute, Mr. Porter—" the cop said.

Julie kept going. Both the cop and I had to hurry to keep up. Doggedly the officer followed.

"I'll have to ask you some questions," he said.

We reached the corner. Julie glanced at the signal, then turned with his bundle of little girl and looked at the cop. "You know my name," he said, "and where I live. I'll be there."

He turned again, waiting for the signal to change. The cop scowled at his back and at me.

"I'm going over to the Hollywood station in a few minutes," I said. "I'll be glad to fill you in, sign the complaints."

He scowled some more, knifed another sidelong glance at Julie's back. The signal changed and Julie stepped off the curb. The cop tried once more.

"Mr. Porter—" Then Linda came into it. In a flash, it was revealed to me who really runs the world. Her white face over her father's shoulder looked mottled under the ill-assorted lights of the busy street. Her eyes seemed a little out of line and there were creases of strain beside her twisted mouth. For a moment she was ageless and eternal—baby, grandmother, woman and crone all in one. But she spoke up very loud and, as always, very clear. "Go away!" she said. "Leave us alone. Go *away*!"

The cop gave her a long look, blinked, then turned and walked away toward the theater. Linda watched him as we crossed the street, then put her head down again. She was a girl and it was part of the business of girls to be rescued. But I had no doubt that, lacking an available knight, she would damn well rescue herself, now and forever.

We found Julie's car in the parking lot and I paid the disgruntled attendant. He suffered an acute attack of righteousness and went into a windy lecture about tickets and identification and I nodded as I walked away.

I looked in at Julie behind the wheel. Linda was lying on the back seat, her eyes fixed on a point in the ceding.

"I'll go talk to the cops," I said.

"You coming out to the house then?"

"Not tonight. I'll go by Reilly's and try to find the money in the car and bring it around tomorrow."

"Take enough out to pay the hospital, huh?"

"All right."

"Come out early, Mac. I want to talk about something." His shrewd eyes worked at mine. "I've been thinking—you're a lot like Bernie was. I need somebody—"

I nudged his arm with my fist. "I'm honored, Julie," I said. "But it's not my kind of work. You'll find somebody."

He stared blankly ahead. His shoulders lifted and fell. "I'd like for Alice Hummel to come back," he said. "I'll make it up to her for—whatever it was."

"If I see her," I said.

"Yeah," he said.

"Good night." I looked into the back seat. "Good night, Linda."

"Good night," she said.

She didn't look at me, just at that place on the ceiling.

* * * *

I took a taxi up into the hills and managed to find the Reilly house. I went over Reilly's car. He had stuck the foil-wrapped package back under the front seat. It was a thick stack of bills of assorted denominations. I didn't take time to count it, but it was all real money, no padding.

There had been a shift change at the hospital and the nurse at the desk apparently hadn't been briefed, so there was no trouble.

"How is he?" I asked.

She looked at some papers.

"Says, 'Dislocation of tracheal cartilage—not critical—sedative—indicate manipulation—'"

"How much?" I asked.

"The established deposit is a hundred dollars," she said.

I had to dig into the payoff package to get it. The nurse, a woman of thirty with big breasts under the starched white uniform, betrayed involuntary interest.

"That's quite a wallet," she said.

I handed her a hundred dollars. She opened a receipt book, poised her pencil over it.

"Make it out to Julian Porter," I said.

She started to write, then looked up quickly. "The producer?" she said.

I nodded.

"You're not—"

"No," I said.

"Well, what's *your* name?"

"It's real money," I said. "Just make it out to Julian Porter."

She looked at her fingernails. "Not even for my own personal reference?" she said.

"My wife and six kids are waiting in the car," I said.

She sighed, made out the receipt and handed it to me.

"Good night," I said.

* * * *

It took me about an hour at the police station. I told the story—most of it—to a stenographer, then waited while it was transcribed and half a dozen detectives and officers read it. Not till the ragged end did they let me know what Louise Reilly had confessed. They wouldn't have let me know then, but I had caught them muttering comparisons between my transcript and another and I tricked a young officer into telling me.

At about one-forty-five in the morning, they released me. A cheerful, middle-aged detective sergeant showed me to an official car.

"I'll give you a lift to your hotel," he said. "Going that way anyhow."

I went along. We spent a little time chatting about police problems, on most of which we saw eye to eye. We were rolling down the Hollywood Freeway toward the Civic Center when he threw me the curve, as I had known he would.

"About this Bernie Wolf," he said, "the Reilly woman claims she killed. What's the rest of it?"

"I think you have all of it," I said.

"He was playing with Porter's wife, wasn't he?"

"Not to my knowledge," I said.

He nudged me in a friendly way. "Come on," he said, "you're leaving town. Wolf is dead, Mrs. Reilly confessed—what can you lose?"

"I don't know what you're talking about."

"You'll be subpoenaed, you know that."

"Possibly."

"So—now or later—what's the difference?"

Bernie had explained it, but Bernie was dead. "I've seen him hurt..."

He would be hurt again. The newspapers would hurt him. I would hurt him myself if I had to go to court, if the question got past the bench, if I had to answer it. But I would not hurt him in the back seat of a shiny car purchased by the taxpayers of Los Angeles County, out of a loose mouth to a strange cop for the dingy sake of a solid-pack case tied with red ribbon. After a few minutes of silence, the sergeant knew I wouldn't.

I let myself out of the car at the hotel and said good night. The sergeant nodded and slammed the door. I looked up at the hotel for a minute, then walked down the street to an all-night restaurant and drank some coffee. The cut on my face started to bleed again and I held a paper napkin over it while I walked back to the hotel and rode up to my floor. I threw the napkin away in a sand-filled ash pot in the corridor and gave it a few moments of thought, not very deep.

The blood was part of me, but it didn't have anything to do with identity. Millions of men had left gallons of blood in every country in the world, but it hadn't made them part of that country, nor the country part of them. And it never would. You had a certain amount of blood in you. If you were lucky, you kept it. Luck was the only method. I had been lucky.

CHAPTER TWENTY-TWO

She was sitting in the dark by the window, just sitting there, waiting; her prim hands in her lap, her ramrod back stiff and straight. In the gray, striped light through the slatted blind, her face was soft, ethereally pretty. She tilted it slowly as I crossed to the bed and sat down.

"I spend a lot of time just wiping blood off you," she said.

I decided she had feline vision.

"It's nothing much," I said. "And everything's all right. And Julie wants you to come back."

"He does?"

After a minute, she got up, heading for the bathroom. The light went on in there and I heard water running into the bowl, the soft sloshing of a cloth. She had left the door slightly ajar and through the crack I saw lingerie hanging on a towel rack—hose, panties, a petite bra, part of a slip. Returning, she paused in the lighted doorway, gauzily revealed under the thin dress.

"I made myself at home," she said. "Do you mind? I had to wash out a few things."

She drew the door nearly shut and came on.

"Very domestic of you," I said. "I don't mind."

The bed lurched gently as she sat down beside me. She had a clean towel in her lap. Her fingers plucked at my chin, tilting my face into position. There was the harsh shock of the cold compress, then slow relief. She dabbed at it expertly. She smelled faintly of soap.

"Is it very bad?" she said. "What happened?"

"Not much. I had to restrain Julie."

"I don't want to hear the details. Only where you hurt."

"Here and there," I said.

She pressed the dry towel against my face.

"You need someone to take care of you for a change," she said.

"Probably. Who doesn't?"

In memory I saw the row of her "things" hanging on the bathroom rack. She was sitting quietly with the towel and cloth in her lap. I wadded them in my hand and stood up. The base of my skull squeezed upward toward my forehead and I dropped the stuff and sat down heavily, my face cupped in my hands. I felt her shift on the bed, a rustling of fabric and flesh, the dry rasp of a zipper. She slid an arm across my shoulders, urged me downward. My face nuzzled her bared breasts, small, warm and stiffly nippled. The rolled-down bodice of her dress nudged at my collarbone. She touched the bruise on my face and I winced.

"Rest," she said. "Make use of me, Mac."

"It's not quite your calling," I said.

"Maybe it is. As between the natural amateur mother, and the professional—the choice is pretty clear."

"About Julie—"

"I can't go back there. He'll find someone. Sophie can fill in for a while. There's a natural mother for you!"

Her fingers stroked at my neck and scalp. The touch and the warmth of her body were working their ancient spell. I felt myself give into it, drowsy, but with a mounting need. In a subtle, almost imperceptible shifting, she moved beneath me. Our faces were close, her eyes glowing flecks in the half-dark. Her mouth opened. We kissed a long time. She was sweet, virginal to touch and taste.

"Mac—" she whispered. "Help me."

I kissed her again and she moved suddenly, awkwardly, the bed surging under us, pulling her skirt up over her thighs, beyond her hips, bunching it at her waist. I could feel her heart thudding in her naked breast. My hand traveled mechanically, grazed at her, found the taut, untried flesh, held a moment as she tried in swift panic to turn away, then let her go. She lay rigid beside me.

"I can't help you," I said. "Not that way."

"No, please—I'm sorry—it was only for a moment. Be patient with me, Mac—"

"I'm all out of help and patience," I said. "Besides, you can do better. You don't have to hang around with me."

I saw her eyes fill and looked away.

"My God," she said harshly. "How could I—?"

"It was my fault," I said.

"No, it wasn't, but if it helps, let it be that way. You'll have enough to think about without this."

The bedsprings clanged furtively as she rearranged her dress. Then a silence.

"What did you say?" she asked finally.

"You found something," I said. "The night Carol came to my room. You had found the rubber stamp outfit in her room. Your fingers were stained by it, the way Carol's were stained when I found her at Bernie's. That's what she came to tell me, that she had taken it and that it was missing. Then she didn't tell me. And you didn't tell me—almost, but not quite."

"No—I didn't know what it meant. I didn't want to get Carol in trouble—"

"It was the one thing I needed. I couldn't put things together, the dirty fingers weren't enough. If you had told me, right then, that night, I could have put it together. I'd have known—that Bernie didn't tell me because he knew how it would hurt Julie. Bernie thought he could deal with Louise quietly and get it over with—"

"Louise!"

"Sure, Louise. You're disappointed? You wanted it to be Carol, didn't you? You tried to make it be Carol."

"Mac—you talk to me like that? After what I risked coming here—leaving my job—"

"You risked Linda."

"No!" She got off the bed and her body was like a drawn bow in front of me. "When Carol came to your room, I was furious—shameless. I listened at the door, but I couldn't hear what you were saying. I imagined all sorts of things, driving myself crazy! The next thing I knew, there was Julie, the three of you, and then you were packing to leave."

"I see," I said. "All right."

"I didn't know where you would go, and I was afraid to leave Linda. But then later, I thought she would be all right. Honestly I did. Her father was home—Sophie—there was Walewski within reach—" Wearily, stiffly, she made her way to the chair and sat on the edge of it.

"If your things are dry," I said, "I'll take you home."

She looked at me. A car honked brutally down in the street.

"Home," she said bitterly. "A little girl, and Sophie, and—him, Julie—"

"You could do worse than Julie," I said. "He needs a woman—young, like you, competent. He's saved his money. Even if his business dies under him, he'll be all right. You could like Julie, when you understand him. He wants you back."

"Shut up, Mac," she said. "I'll go back. Because—where else? But don't throw me away."

I watched the rise and fall of her virgin breasts, spasmodic and painful.

"If you ask me now," she said, "I'll do it. Or anything. I'll get on the bed and do anything you say and this time I won't get scared. But don't give me away to Julie, Mac, or to anybody else."

"I'm asking you to go back and take care of Linda," I said. "And the next time you get to Chicago, give me a ring."

She sat there for about a minute, her eyes probing the dark, then she went into the bathroom and closed the door. I sat on the bed, waiting. There was a slender, shallow depression where she had been lying.

When she came out, she was brushed and primped and respectably concealed.

"I'm sorry I was so long," she said. "I cried for a while."

"Good for you," I said.

"Shall we go?"

At the door she hung back. "Did he say that really? Does he want me back?"

"Last thing he said to me," I told her.

She turned her small face up, childlike. "Kiss me goodbye, Mac," she said.

I kissed her cheek and her mouth. She smiled. As she walked ahead of me down the hall, she was doing very well. I was proud of her. I thought about her with Linda and Julie in the big house and the years falling away, but it wasn't a picture I could hold onto. It kept coming apart. They would have to work it out some way, some day...